Why We Never Talk About Sugar

WHY WE NEVER TALK ABOUT SUGAR

Stories by Aubrey Hirsch

BRADDOCK
AVENUE
BOOKS
UNCOMMON BOOKS UNCOMMON READERS

Printed in the United States of America
10 9 8 7 6 5 4 3 2 1

FIRST EDITION, March 2013

ISBN-10: 0-615-74179-7
ISBN-13: 978-0-615-74179-6

Acknowledgment is made to the following publcations, in which these stories originally appeared, some differently titled or in a slightly different form: *Annalemma*: "Paradise Hardware" (as "Elysian"); *Bluestem*: "Pinocchio"; *Cedars*: "The News and What it Means to Noah"; *Confrontation*: "No System for Blindness"; *flatmancrooked*: "Made in Indonesia"; *Hobart*: "The Borovsky Circus goes to Littlefield"; *Kaleidoscope*: "Strategy #13: Journal"; *LITSNACK*: "The Snakeskin"; *PANK*: "Certainty," "Hydrogen Event in a Bubble Chamber"; *Pittsburgh Noir*: "Cheater"; *Vestal Review*: "Why We Never Talk About Sugar"; *Whiskey Island Magazine*: "The Specialists." "Leaving Seoul," "Advice for Dealing with the Loss of a Beloved Pet," and "The Disappearance of Maliseet Lake" were not previously published.

Braddock Avenue Books
PO Box 502
Braddock, PA 15204

Cover art by Carter Hodgkin, www.carterhodgkin.com
Book design by Joel W. Coggins

www.braddockavenuebooks.com

For Cal, my other dream come true.

CONTENTS

· · · · · · · · · · · · · · · · · ·

Why We Never Talk About Sugar

Leaving Seoul

. . . .

My body knew I was looking at Kara before my mind did. Before I could conjure up her name, my glands had spiked my blood with adrenaline, a cocktail so potent I had to put my Black Shandy down on the table or risk emptying its contents onto my laptop. I was in a cyber café in Hongdae uploading lessons for my students. What Kara was doing in South Korea, I had no idea.

Though I often imagined I saw her, walking the streets of Seoul, appearing out of the crowd like an apparition, this time it was real. It would have been impossible not to notice her. She was easily six inches taller than everyone around her and probably the only natural blond in the district. A cluster of teenagers followed her with camera phones as if she were a television actress or a Kpop star.

A crowd had also surrounded her the first time I'd seen her—outside a market in Dongjak. Thinking she must be some kind of celebrity, I followed her to the subway, dodging bicyclists and old ladies pushing grocery carts. I sat next to her, asked her the time. "You're American!" she said, flashing a toothpaste-commercial smile. I rode the subway six exits farther than I needed to while we chatted. By the time I finally got home the popsicles I'd bought had turned to juice, but I had a date with her that night.

We met in Bucheon for chilly chicken and sam gyal sal. She told me she was living in Osaka, teaching English to Japanese teenagers. She was visiting South Korea while the kids were on break. I offered to be her tour guide.

"How long have you been here?" she asked

"It'll be four years in March."

"That's a long time. Most Americans go abroad for a year. Maybe two if they like it. You must *really* like it."

I snorted into my beer. The truth was I'd been dreaming about leaving almost since I'd gotten to Seoul. Like Kara I'd come to teach English and have some adventure. It turns out I wasn't really up for it. The streets were too crowded, the air too filthy, the food too spicy or sour. The other teachers in my program were West Coast trust-funders who read Yates and knitted. I was a community college graduate who'd never been outside of southern Ohio for longer than an afternoon. Staring down the barrel of life-long labor at minimum wage, I instead boarded a plane for the farthest place I could think to go: Seoul, South Korea.

My contract promised me airfare home at the end of the year, but the school fired me a month before the term ended, which absolved them from fulfilling their promise. After my rage subsided I calmed down by telling myself I'd find another job, save every won and get myself back home to Ohio by the first of the year.

I soon found I could earn decent money teaching in the

2

illegal after-hours Hagwons, cram-schools for Korean students with achievement-obsessed parents. I applied for a tourist visa and hopped a short flight to China or Japan every three months, got my visa stamped, and flew back. It took a chunk out of my savings, but kept my alien status legal.

What I couldn't stand, though, were the constant raids by South Korean curfew enforcers. At least twice a month we were caught, books open, chalk in hand, and forced to shut down until we could find a new location, usually above a restaurant or a laundry. After one raid that kept us closed for more than a week, a former co-teacher tipped me off to a way to make just as much money with less time and less risk, uploading lessons and study sheets online. Parents paid a few hundred thousand won for membership and you never even had to be in the same room as a kid who was violating his study curfew. The work was easy. I did my uploads from business centers and cyber cafés and kept under the radar.

It would have worked like a charm except that to steady my nerves until I could get home, I'd developed a pack a day addiction to Korean clove cigarettes. When I went more than a couple of hours without one, my head would pound and my hands would shake. Sometimes I got diarrhea. More often I vomited. By the time I'd saved enough money for a trip to the states, I couldn't even sit through a long movie without becoming ill. There was simply no way I could let the nicotine drain out of my body for six hours while I waited for an airplane to cross an ocean.

My new plan, I told Kara during our first meeting, was to take an eighty-three day, open-air cruise that traveled from Yokohama to Los Angeles. Now I just needed to save the money.

"How much have you got?" she asked.

"About five million won."

Her eyes widened.

"Don't get too excited," I said. "That's only a few thousand bucks." Her glass was empty, so I poured her another beer. "How long are you staying?"

"I was only planning a week or so. But apparently, plans can change," she said, then that smile again.

At some point it became obvious that we would spend the night together. We took the subway back to my apartment in Seocho. Her body was round and warm. We stayed up the whole night, talking and touching each other. She wore a jade charm around her neck that bobbed an inch from my nose when she climbed on top of me. She said it was lucky. I told her I thought it might be catching.

••••

She was still wearing it when she came into the cyber café in Hongdae, though it had been more than two years since that night. My eyes were drawn to it and before I could look away, she'd turned in my direction. It's a kind of sixth sense, isn't it? That thing that makes your skin prickle when someone in the room is watching you?

It was the lack of exactly this kind of instinct, no doubt, that had made me such an easy mark for Kara. Her affection seemed genuine. At no point did I even begin to suspect that she was setting me up for a huge loss and, in the meantime, sentencing me to another three years in polluted South Korea.

She had been careful and thoughtful with her scam. The whole thing took less than two weeks. For the first, we were inseparable. I took her sightseeing. We picnicked at Gyeongbok Palace, taking awkward self portraits with the camera held at arm's lengths and my armpit foregrounded in the frame. We went to clubs where we stayed out until morning and drank until we couldn't dance anymore. There was sex also, lots of it. She never refused me.

Then she disappeared.

For four days I called and texted. I sent her emails and spent long hours outside her apartment, sucking down cigarettes and watching for her. I thought about trying to get in touch with her parents or the police. It sounds like an over-reaction, I'm sure, but the infatuation was strong. We hadn't been away from each other for more than an hour or two since we'd met and I was beginning to feel the same way I felt when I tried, futilely, to cut out the Indigos for a day. Finally, when I felt on the edge of sanity, she replied to one of my emails suggesting we meet for dinner in a little restaurant across the street from her subway exit.

My stomach flipped itself inside out as I waited for her to arrive. What would she say? Had she discovered something unpleasant about me? Had she met someone else? Had there been someone else all along, waiting for her in Japan perhaps, and the guilt was finally bubbling over into action?

When Kara showed up her blond hair was hidden under a navy knit cap. The pieces that poked out of the back looked unwashed. Her eyes were puffy, her lips cracked. As she worked the buttons on her black coat I could see that she'd bitten all of her fingernails down to bloody splinters. The fact that I didn't immediately ask what was wrong shows that maybe I did have some instincts toward self-preservation after all. What I saw before me was the embodiment of grief, a pit I did not want to be sucked into. I stayed quiet, forcing her to speak first.

"I," she began, immediately interrupting herself with an unscripted "oh my god." A long sip of water seemed to steady her and she continued. "I'm pregnant."

I think back on this moment often and while I'm sure I must have been feeling something at the time, I can't for the life of me access that feeling. I like to think of myself as someone who's good in a crisis, but here I reverted to a reaction lifted from sitcom teleplays. I asked, "Are you sure?"

"Why do people ask that? Of course I'm sure. I've taken twelve tests in four days."

"Are you sure you understood the instructions? Some-

5

times I'm not even sure how to eat candy bars in this country." I tried to let out a little laugh to lighten the mood, but choked on it.

"The instructions were in English."

She broke into a series of quiet, controlled sobs that kept me from asking any more questions. Instead I waited for her to tell me what to do and, eventually, she did.

"I can't have it, obviously," she said.

I nodded. All I could feel was relief. The guilt would come later.

She insisted on going to Sweden for the actual procedure. Though not uncommon in South Korea, abortions were technically illegal. She didn't feel good about her prospects in Osaka either. Kara said a well-traveled friend of hers had once had one in Stockholm and that she'd felt comfortable there.

I agreed to help any way I could and in the end that meant buying her a flight to Stockholm, a week in a private room in a hostel while she recovered, and another plane ticket from Stockholm directly back to Japan. It wouldn't make sense, she said, for her to come back to Seoul when it was over. "Maybe I'll come back another time," she said, but we both knew she wouldn't. A thing like this just soured everything.

It wasn't until a week or so after she left, my bank account drained, that I started to sense that something may have been amiss. A quick internet search revealed no reason to avoid having the procedure in Japan. This discovery made me think more carefully about the timing of the events as she had presented it to me. Was it possible for her to get a positive pregnancy test only one week after the first time we slept together? Apparently it was technically possible, though unlikely. But surely she would know that, if she were running a scam. She would make sure there was just enough time so that her story wouldn't be easily debunked. I should have asked to see the pregnancy test, or better yet, go to a clinic with her and see the tiny fluttering heartbeat with my own eyes, if there even was one. Why hadn't I asked?

Once I finished my research I was convinced that the whole thing had been a lie. Not just the pregnancy, but the sex, too. And the hand-holding. And the long kisses on the subway surrounded by disapproving eyes. I wondered if her name was really Kara. I wondered how many times she'd done this. How many free trips around the world she'd racked up at the expense of suckers like me.

I couldn't decide which was worse: the idea that I'd gotten her pregnant and she'd undone it, or the idea that I hadn't. I sunk myself into my work. I put more effort into recruiting students. I sucked down Indigos with renewed vigor, leaving long lines of ash on the surfaces around my apartment like ghosts of cigarettes. I set myself a new timeline. In three years I'd either have enough money to take the ship back to America, or I'd have kicked the nicotine habit that was keeping me chained to this crowded city, seemingly a million miles from home.

••••

After locking eyes with me for a moment, Kara glanced at the door, where the group of teenaged boys were still pressing their noses against the glass, and then back at me. When she got her drink, she set it down on the table across from me. I noticed it was in a to-go cup, probably she needed to be ready to make a quick getaway. "Hey there," she said, sitting down. I closed my laptop and shoved it into my bag under the table.

"You're still doing that, huh?"

Kara saw my part in the cram-school culture as something utterly illicit. "It's just like child pornography," she'd said. "You're hunched over your little laptop in the dingy coffee house. You're totally exploiting those kids. The study curfews are there for a reason, you know."

This time shutting down her judgmental tone was easy. "I have to make some money. I got cleaned out of my savings a while back." It came out like a dagger. I was still angry. The amount of anger surprised me. "How was Sweden?"

I'd meant it as a barb, but Kara's stoic expression didn't even wobble. "You'll be glad to know that I've put all that behind me. I don't do that anymore."

"And you've come to give my money back?"

She waved her hand and cracked a toothless smile. "So far behind me. I don't even think about it."

"I suppose I was the last one, right? The one that made you realize you needed to change your life?"

"No," she said, she blew briefly on her coffee as if her concentrated breath would cool it instantly. "There were two after you. One in Morocco, one in Egypt."

Her sincerity caught me off guard. Her voice was so hollow I almost pitied her. I had to remind myself that this was what Kara did. This was what got her from country to country. This conjuring of sympathy. This architecture of untruths. This was how Kara lived.

"I won't bore you with my justifications," she said. "It was wrong."

It occurred to me that she might have come to Seoul looking for me, that I might be part of some elaborate endeavor to clear her karma. "Why are you in Korea?" I asked.

"Just a vacation," she said. "I have fond memories of this place." She took a sip of her coffee, leaving pink lip gloss on the rim of her cup. "I thought you'd be long gone by now."

"No," I said.

"Since you're here, I want to say something, even if you can't believe it. I am sorry about everything that happened."

I was tempted to roll my eyes at her or, if I had been a different kind of person, to deck her, right on her perfect, freckled nose. If I was going to do something vengeful, this was the moment. It was probably the only moment I'd ever have. If any part of me had expected it, it may have gone differently. But in the end, after these strange years filled with deception and doubt, I had to decide that I wasn't risking much by being genuine for a moment, and maybe allowing myself to be fooled one last time. "Me too," I said. It was the truest thing I could think to say.

She nodded firmly, only once, and picked up her paper cup. "I guess I should go." If she was waiting for me to stop her, she'd be waiting a long time. "I hope you get back home soon," she said.

After she left I smoked and watched the window for a while, studying the people hurrying past. I wondered if home was the place you tried to get to or the place you tried to leave.

The Borovsky Circus Goes to Littlefield

●●●

Sandeep

The tiger is beautiful. A vision. Sandeep, the big cat trainer, thinks it moves like Jharkhand wind, like a bee-eater in the Tallgrass, all teeth and twitching tail. He can trace its ancestry back to the Mughal Dynasty when its forbearers were kept as pets to please the Emperor. For generations, these tigers have been bred and trained for one thing: entertainment.

But now the star tiger sleeps all day. His companions, also Bengals, do the same. Sometimes one will anemically chase another. Sometimes the largest male will leap without purpose, as if through a flaming hoop. But none win a treat. There are no more treats to be won.

Originally from India, Sandeep came with the circus

from Russia for a two-year, forty-city tour across the Western United States. They were billed as The Great Baker Circus, though at home they are called The Borovsky Circus. There are clowns, gymnasts, jugglers, aerial artists, and a menagerie of animals whose native lands span the globe: Indian tigers, African elephants, Russian horses, hulking Canadian bears, German toy poodles that stand on top of one another like oranges in a crate.

Three cities into their tour, the promoters have pulled their money. Far from the peaceful snowdrifts of Moscow and even farther from the lush green forests of Dalma, the circus is stuck in the arid Texas desert. The performers and trainers did not know this could happen. Their contract was in English. Between them they speak most languages, but they only read Russian, Mandarin, Swedish, a little Cantonese and Urdu. The lawyer translated the basics of what they were signing. This clause, he did not translate.

On Tuesday, they learned that they weren't moving ahead to Wichita Falls. By Thursday, the utilities companies had shut off the electricity and water to the site of the temporary pavilion. Sandeep and the others wonder when the promoters will send men to disassemble the tent that gives them shelter, pack up the portable toilets, remove the little rooms they rest in, wall by wall. The circus owns the animals, but the cages belong to the promoters.

The animals are the only ones that do not seem worried. The tiger has given up leaping through invisible hoops. He is curled in the corner of his pen.

••••

Udofia

This is the elephant trainer's first time in America. It is hotter than he thought, and dryer. He is used to the thick wet heat of Nigeria. Here, even his skin is thirsty. The Littlefield city council has arranged for water to be brought to the pavilion. Three times a day, it comes in big trucks. Like Udo, the animals are used to freer, easier access to water. They do not thrive within this new system, especially not the elephants who, for the first three days, waste their rations shooting tall streams of water onto each others' backs.

The citizens of Littlefield have not abandoned the circus. And Udo doesn't think they will. They have been mesmerized for twelve shows over seven long days by the circus' juggling and clowns and aerial and equestrian skill and dancing bears and poodle towers. Now they bring hay, big burlap sacks of oats, cans of fancy wet dog food, whole fish for the bears, and raw hamburger, which the tigers eat hungrily, licking the last drops of blood from the concrete floor, though they are used to lamb and goat.

For the performers and trainers, the banquet is even richer: buckets of fried chicken, pulled pork sandwiches with sauce that stings Udo's lips and makes his chin sticky for hours, cool bowls of coleslaw that they eat first so it does not sit in the heat, liters and liters of sweet brown tea. At first Udo longs for the grapefruits and gari dumplings of home. Then he thinks about the curries and rices and stews he's discovered on his travels. This desert food is new, but he learns to love it as well. The tacky feeling on his chin and hands reminds him of the rainy season in Lagos. He wants to rub coleslaw on the elephants' hot backs. *Barbeque.* He learns to pronounce the word perfectly. *Who knew such a thing existed?*

••••

Maksim

Of course, their extended picnic cannot go on forever. At last the men come to take the tent away. They spend five days de-rigging, un-tying, re-rolling, and tightly packing the pavilion into big white trucks. The circus people do not know or ask where the tent is going. They don't try to stop the men, but they don't help them either. Even when two of them struggle to balance the weight of a tall tent pole, Maksim, the strong man, stands tauntingly close but does not help. He lifts his enormous barbells above his head with little effort, rolling his neck this way and that as if the lifting relaxes him.

But all is not lost. The Texans have found them a new home. It may not be ideal, but it is the best they can do. The important things were running water, beds, safe places for the animals. When all other possibilities were exhausted, the Texans helped move the circus into a decommissioned women's prison just outside of town. In many ways it is perfect. They sleep two to a room, just like in the circus caravan. They leave their doors wide open so it doesn't feel like prison. The cells are small, but no one suffers from claustrophobia— especially not the clowns. The tigers are locked up tight on the second floor. They take turns jumping in and out of the empty bed frame. The bears, one to a room, stay on the ground level. The elephants, too big for cells, roam the emptied gym. They make a horrifying mess, which their trainer diligently cleans.

For Maksim, the prison feels too much like home. For years he ping-ponged off the walls of a jail in Norilsk. He woke up with the chills, balled beneath his thin grey blanket. To pass the time and generate heat, he did thousands of push-ups a day. He turned his bed frame on end and did pull-ups for hours. When he left Norilsk he was twice the man he was when he arrived. Now, he has no chills. The thick Texas heat crawls into the windows and he wakes up covered in sweat. When he gets too hot, he closes his cell door and imagines he is back in that other prison, unable to escape. It never fails to cool him down. Behind the silver bars, he can feel the chilly Russian air in his teeth.

....

Li

Every night Li prays for a solution. They cannot live in the prison forever. The Texans have already lost their friendly smiles when they pass around platters of cold cuts. The animals need exercise, structure. Something must be done; they need to make money. Li is the most experienced acrobat. He is the only one who can do a double somersault with a double twist and finish by grabbing the long white pole with his outstretched hands, his body straight as a board and perfectly parallel to the ground. As the de facto leader, he understands that the onus is his.

For three days he hangs upside down from a decommissioned gas line in his open cell. He believes that this will help him think by sending all the blood to his brain. Li has done all of his best thinking upside down. Sometimes when he is completing a tumbling series, he catches single moments of pure understanding. He can almost grab them, and then he is right side up again and they are gone. He flips as fast as he can. He knows that if he can rotate fast enough, the moments will connect, like a flipbook.

Again, the inverted position works. Li has an idea. He calls the group together to reveal it. He speaks in Mandarin, *We will put on the circus.* Another acrobat translates it into Russian. The strong man translates from Russian to Urdu. A clown from Urdu to Hindi. A stagehand from Hindi to Thai. Slowly, the idea trickles through the crowd. Smiles break like falling dominoes. It makes Li think of Pentecost, when the Holy Spirit bestowed on the apostles the ability to speak in tongues. He learned about it in an underground religious service, before fleeing China for good. He watches as relief washes over the crowd. Their voices rise in a flurry of languages. Where Li is standing, it sounds like gibberish, but he can tell by the joy on their faces that it is rapture.

Dahlia

It takes an hour and a half for Dahlia, who only understands Swedish, to find someone who can translate Li's plan for her. When she finally does, she rushes out to the prison yard to join the others. They are scrutinizing what will become their new performance venue. The yard is a long rectangle with rounded edges. A five-lane track runs the perimeter. Surrounding the track is a wire fence, at least seven meters high, topped by a nest of razor wire that sparkles in the Texas sun. The space inside the track is divided into three sections: a basketball court, a grassy area, and a tennis court with no net.

To Dahlia's eyes, the place was made for a down-on-its-luck three-ring circus. She can already see it transformed. *Ladies and Gentlemen, please direct your attention to the center ring, where Klemens and his Amazing Poodles are gearing up for another spirited performance. Meanwhile, in the first ring, Cong and Quang show off their skill: juggling burning batons for your amusement. In the third ring, we have Elephants on Parade! Everyone shout hello to Mogi, our newest elephant addition!*

The spectators, she imagines, will be nestled between the tall wire fence and the even taller concrete wall ten meters behind it. This way, no scheming teenagers with binoculars will be able to see the show for free. The wire fence will keep children from running toward the elephants, and protect the spectators should the tigers grow weary of their hamburger.

Dahlia will string her high wire from fencepost to fencepost across all three rings. Sure, seven meters isn't very high. She's used to working at twenty meters, without a net. But it's certainly high enough to be dangerous, were she to fall onto the blacktop of the basketball court below. She can already hear the crowd gasping, shouting things she can't understand in their slow Texas accents. And the view from over the wall—how many prisoners longed for that view?—will be a private joy, something secret just for her.

．．．．

Klemens

Rehearsals commence. Klemens, the poodle trainer, who is from Austria by way of London and speaks perfect English, doesn't think anyone will show. *These are Americans!* he insists. *They do not spend their free time visiting prisons.* Or circuses, he thinks, for that matter. If they did, the promoters wouldn't have pulled out in the first place. But the Texans say they've sold many tickets. The circus people hope not only to pay their living expenses, but to save up enough money to return to Russia, where they have their own cages, their own bathrooms, their own permanent pavilion.

At the dress rehearsal on Thursday night, Klemens becomes even more afraid. The promoters have taken their lighting, the colorful bases on which the elephants do their balancing act, the elaborate costumes. In the prison yard, the performers wear their old costumes, from shows they performed in Russia. While they used to suffice, Klemens cannot believe they ever appeared in them in public. His own ridiculous blue suit is threadbare and too short at the ankles. The orange stripes on each leg are missing sequins. He looks at his shoes and cannot see his reflection. In place of the blue-tinted spotlight that used to follow him around the center ring, there is the floodlight from the top of the tall fence. It stays fixed, and he must guide his poodles into the single beam of light. His is not the only act that suffers. The acrobats have no trapeze. They throw tumbling passes across the basketball court, moving and twisting in and out of the light. The jugglers' costumes do not match. The tigers leap through candy-colored hula-hoops. The elephants balance on overturned washtubs.

Worst of all, there is no music. For Klemens, the music is what turns the disparate oddities of the circus to magic. It hides the poodles' yipping. It hides the strong man's labored breathing. It makes everything feel effortless; it turns awkward movement into dancing. In the bright, colored spotlights Klemens cannot see anything. The music is what guides him. He can feel it filling him in a way that no amount of tangy pulled pork sandwiches ever could.

When it is his turn to practice his performance, he hums to the poodles a song he learned in Austria. As the first four poodles form their solid line for the poodle tower, he adds in the words, slowly. He cannot believe he remembers them. The second row climbs up and he is really singing. When the next two poodles form the third layer he is almost shouting: *Auf die Erde nieder, wo wir Menschen sind!* Finally, Millie, hops to the top and settles in. Klemens, light headed from his singing, looks at the tower. It is brilliant, even without the poodles' miniature golden fezzes. The poodles are centered in the single floodlight, which electrifies Klemens's trousers, sending little explosions of color up and down his legs as he moves to the music. Everything is light and fullness. Klemens bows deeply, signals his poodles to the wings. He jogs off, still singing, and doesn't stop until he is back in his cell. He knows he'll need a good night's sleep to be ready for the opening tomorrow.

••••

Pich

As promised, there is a wonderful turnout for Friday night's performance. The tickets go for seven dollars for adults, five dollars for children and senior citizens. They are American dollars and Pich is not sure of their value, but the others assure him it is a lot of money. The Texans bring lawn chairs and folding wooden stools. Some of them spread out blankets and recline on the grass. Others stand, leaning against the thick concrete wall.

Pich is excited to perform, even though his stage time has been cut by nearly two thirds. When they had backers, the clowns' act started with all twelve of them pouring out of a green Volkswagen Beetle, whose seats, steering column and engine had been removed. They ran around a bit, tripping over nothing, squirting each other with oversized bottles of seltzer. Then they all queued up for a choreographed pogo stick routine, ending with synchronized back layouts. Now there are no pogo sticks, no giant seltzer bottles, no gutted Volkswagen Beetle. Now there is only the tripping, the over-sized shoes, the faded organza collars.

The light comes on and the clowns enter the first ring. They have a new bit where they pretend to be fighting over the one-meter diameter of the single spotlight. This comforts Pich. He thinks they are adapting. He thinks it is a good sign. It is not quite dark and he can see a few meters in every direction. He is not used to seeing his audience as he performs. Usually they are hidden away in the darkness, out of reach of his pinprick pupils, chewing cotton candy and slurping sodas. But here they are, the Americans, right in front of him.

The sight of them rattles Pich so that he is no longer fighting for the spotlight with the other clowns. He lets himself get pushed out of the way and now fights for an understanding of what has happened to the circus. It occurs to him that the audience members look like *they* are in prison, trapped behind the wire fence. Some of the children poke their fingers through the chain links. Some are climbing the fence. Their parents pull them down by their waistbands, pointing to the razor wire at the top. But Pich knows that the Americans are not in prison. At any time, they can move out from between the fences and into the desert air. They will go back to their homes with their real rooms and beds and familiar foods. But what awaits Pich beyond the tall prison gates? He can think of nothing. His prison, he knows, is this one in Littlefield, but it is a metaphorical one as well.

••••

Tamara

Despite the myriad improvisations, the shows at the prison go so well that the crowds are bigger every night. A Littlefield news station writes a review, then a Texas newspaper picks up the story, and finally, a national news outlet covers it and a wealthy gentleman in Montana agrees to back the circus for the rest of its pre-planned tour and one televised special. The Borovsky Circus will earn enough money to send themselves back to Russia and then, well, who knows what then? On their last night in Littlefield, they put on a free show, open to the public, to thank their generous Texan hosts. After the show, they celebrate. They take turns pointing at the map and imagining the cities they'll visit.

Tamara, an acclaimed equestrian artist, does not join them. Like the others, she is glad to be moving on from Littlefield, but she is leaving someone behind. Her horse, Kostya, a thoroughbred and an albino, has been devastatingly injured. *He needs to be re-shoed each month*, she told the others. But there was no money for shoes. As a result, Kostya split a hoof and the resulting fall dislocated his knee. It happened during the week, when the circus performers rest and practice. The equestrian act was performed on Friday night, as always, but without Tamara and Kostya. Nobody noticed.

A Texan man is supposed to be sheltering him in his barn while he recovers, but Tamara, who does not speak English and could not understand his low whispering voice, suspects that Kostya has already been put down. Her horse is her act, her life. Without him, she knew she could not contribute to the show. The other performers asked Tamara to come along with them still. They found jobs for her to do: feeding the poodles, cleaning up after the elephants, sewing sequins onto costumes in the laundry truck of their new caravan. She is an artist, a talented rider, not a laundry girl. Her leg muscles ache for a full and sustained straddle. Sometimes she finds herself posting, from her knees, as she scoops dry food into the poodles' bowls. She does this to keep from weeping. She is no idiot. She knows where dog food comes from.

Tamara is not the only one whose unhappiness will follow her out of Littlefield. As she goes from room to room gathering laundry, she sees hints of gloom. It lurks beneath the clowns' pink make-up. It is in the almost imperceptible under-rotation of the once brilliant acrobats. She can see it in the way the tigers have stopped growling and now preen themselves like kittens. The poodle-trainer sings to himself constantly. The tightrope walker has requested a thicker wire.

When Tamara feeds the poodles, no one applauds. No one throws roses. It is a big change, and she finds it difficult to adjust. After the tour, Tamara will be done with the circus for good. While they move from city to city, she will think only of Russia, where she can be back in Latonovo on a horse on her cousin's farm. She will learn to exist without the fancy costumes, the feathery rows of fake eyelashes, the sizzling heat of the spotlight. On the farm, she will feed the animals and fold the laundry. Some nights she might begin to imagine that she is back in Texas, in the circus, Kostya's warm bulk beneath her, but she will always stop this. She will never allow herself to go back there.

Pinocchio

· · · · · · · · · · ·

Now that Pinocchio is finally a real boy, he understands that what he really wants to be is a woman. He knows he has to tell his father, Geppetto, who spent his whole life longing for a son.

"Dad," he says, "I need to talk to you about something." He looks around his father's small house. It seems much smaller now that Pinocchio is grown up. From the kitchen, he can see Geppetto's studio, littered with puppets flung about like tiny dead bodies. "You know what you always say about making the puppets? That you can tell what's inside the chunk of pine even before you start carving it? That you just *know*?"

Geppetto nods. He carries a basket of bread to the table with arthritic fingers.

"I know something, too," Pinocchio says. "About what I

am inside." He tells Geppetto that although he gave him the features of a boy and a boy's name, he guessed wrong when he picked up this particular piece of pine.

Geppetto stays quiet as Pinocchio speaks. When he's finished, he asks, "How long have you known?"

Pinocchio considers it for a moment. It's a difficult question to answer. It's possible that, on some level, he has always known. At the very least, he's always felt like an intruder in his own body. When he was a child, it was easy to attribute his discomfort to the fact that he was made of wood. He wasn't like the other boys. He would study himself in the mirror for hours imagining a different body, thinking about being a different person.

When the wood was changed for skin, it didn't get any better. He thought he just needed to get used to this new form. But, no, this wasn't right either. In response to his dad's question he just shrugs. "A while," he says. "I didn't know how to tell you."

"Is this because you never had a mother?" Geppetto asks.

"No," says Pinocchio, but it kind of makes sense now that he's thinking about it. He doesn't think it would have changed anything, but if he'd been around women more, maybe he would have realized it earlier. Growing up, there was only him, his father, the cricket, the cat, and the fish—all men.

Geppetto shakes his head. "Maybe I didn't socialize you properly."

Pinocchio remembers the first time he met other boys, real boys. They were drunks and gamblers. They smoked big cigars and smelled like sweat and cotton candy. *Is this what it means*, he wondered, *to be a man?*

"It's no one's fault," Pinocchio says. "Because there's nothing to be upset about. This is who I am inside. This is how you made me."

On the way back home after dinner, Pinocchio thinks about all the men that he's met in his life and the fever they built, collectively, in his heart. Jiminy and Figaro and Cleo are all dead. He doesn't know what's become of Monstro, the whale that scared him three quarters to death, or the boys that changed to donkeys. And then there is his father, his father's slow, shaking head. The way his father's face says, *All I ever wanted was for you to be a real boy.* If he were still made of wood, he'd be broken or burnt by now.

It isn't any wonder, then, that he hallucinates a curvy blond with full pink lips to play his subconscious. *Pinocchio,* she whispers into his ear like a lullaby, *this is who you are inside.* In his dreams, when she takes off her clothes, he doesn't touch her. He looks at her, studying each inch for a full minute for the entire time he is asleep.

Pinocchio wishes he could have her soft skin and long hair. He wishes for her tiny, perfect teeth. He wishes his father would say he understands. Say, *You're the child I always wanted.* But more than anything he wishes for a time when he doesn't have to wish anymore.

Strategy #13: Journal
● ●

My father is bringing my mother breakfast in bed even though it is not her birthday, and then he is calling her a heartless bitch just loud enough for us to hear.

Elapsed time: nine years.

This all started when my dad was diagnosed with multiple sclerosis. He doesn't mean any of the terrible things he says. It's the damaged brain myelin talking. My mother doesn't mean what she says, either. It's misplaced anger. Trust me, I know all about it. I can refer you to literature on the topic.

When the doctors can't cure you, they bury you in brochures. Waiting room walls are covered with them. They all have uplifting names like: *Creating a Happy Life*, *Fighting the Crazies*, *Food for Thought: Nutrition and MS*, and my favorite, *Keep S'myelin*. Red is procedures. Orange is diet. Yellow is talking to your family. Green is alternate procedures. Blue is managing your symptoms. Purple is the most basic. This brochure, *MS and You* is the first brochure I ever read and the laminated label on the wall below it read: Information. Now, my brother and I are upstairs reading it for the thousandth time.

The brochure says: "Myelin is like the covering on a cord that sends computer messages from your brain to your nerves. Multiple Sclerosis damages this covering. The scars left by the damage act like a computer virus that slows down important information. This is why certain tasks are difficult to perform."

My brother says, "Practical knowledge for the internet generation. Fucking lame."

I say, "It's meant for little kids, Mark."

"It's fucking lame."

The brochure says, "It is normal to feel angry at the disease."

Downstairs, I can hear my mother saying "You're tired all the time, Dan! I want to be like other couples. I want to go out to movies. I want to go out to dinner."

When my father was finally diagnosed, I think she took it sort of personally. Maybe she thinks he got the better end of the deal because he doesn't have to watch someone he loves waste away.

Through clenched teeth, my dad says, "Yeah. You really have it hard, Madelyn. I'd hate to be in your shoes."

The brochure contains a strategy guide outlining coping strategies for people with MS, and their family members.

Strategy #1: Be Patient.

"There's nothing in here about what to do when everyone stops loving each other," Mark says.

The brochure says, "Your family members are able to love and support you whether or not they have MS."

My mother says, "I want to go dancing, Dan."

25

My dad says, "Then go dance, Lyn."

My mother says, "I need to get out of here. You make this whole place feel sick."

My dad says, "Go."

A door slams.

The brochure tells us, "It is normal to feel angry at the person who has MS."

Mark looks at me and I look away.

The brochure says, "Be honest and open about your feelings."

I don't say anything.

••••

My mother is always leaving like that, and she leaves for good the next week. Almost a year later the divorce is being finalized. Mark's gone away to college and rarely calls because he's too busy trading coke for term papers.

Strategy #14: Try New Things.

My mother calls me so I'll forgive her for walking out on my dad. And on me.

"I know it's going to be hard for you."

"Well, thanks for all your help," I say.

"There's no possible way I can make you understand how much this hurts."

I think, not as much as sticking around. But I don't say that.

I say, "I can imagine how I'd feel if I ran out on dad."

I can hear my father's voice in my head saying, "I'd sure hate to be in your shoes."

"You see what it does to me. I'm not strong enough for this. I yell. I get angry."

"But it's important that you're there."

"I'd be making things worse," she says. "Trust me. You and Mark will be much more caring. And understanding."

I tell her that Mark is gone. That it is just me.

I say, "Your faith is overwhelming. Really, it's too much."

"It's different for you, honey. It's not that you don't love him as much. That's not what makes it easier. Parents and children always mean the world to each other, no matter what. But it's different for me and him."

"Yeah," I say, "apparently."

"I don't expect you to understand this now. I know you love him. But I picked him."

What a cop-out.

"Don't expect me to understand this ever," I say.

And there it is, the perfect hang up line. But I don't take it. I want her to convince me that she really does love him still and that it really is better this way and that everything will all work out. Please, mom.

But she just says, "I'd better go. Think about what I said. If you need anything, you know to call."

I think, yeah, I need a wife for my father.

I say, "Yeah. Bye."

....

I remember my father ending my time-outs early so we could play together. Now he is crying loudly in his bedroom for the sixth straight day.

He isn't really sad about anything. It's just side effects from the medication. Nausea, Fatigue, Depression. You have no idea.

I cross to the bathroom to plug in the curling iron and the noise stops. My dad stumbles into the living room and falls into the couch.

"Hun?"

"Yeah dad," I say.

"What are your plans tonight?"

This almost always means he needs something. A ride to

the grocery store, or to the emergency room. He needs me to give him his shot, read a recipe card, reach something high, or to change a light bulb.

Tonight is my friend's party, but I don't say that.

"Nothing really. Why?"

"I just thought you might want to play a game of chess later."

This is the first time my dad has left his bedroom in almost a week, and it's the first time he's asked me for a game of chess in over a month. So I try not to think about what I want. But it creeps into my head anyway. I'd been looking forward to this party for a month, and I'd told my dad about it at least four times.

On the surface of my brain I'm glad he's awake and somewhat energized. I want him to feel like this. I want him to lie on the couch with me and watch old eighties music videos. But the just underneath part of my brain wants him to go to sleep and not need anything so I can be with my friends. And I'll play chess with him tomorrow. As many times as he wants.

Strategy #2: Take Time for Yourself.

That's just the kind of selfish bitch I am. Like mother, like daughter. But there are some things you cannot bargain with. I unplug the curling iron.

"Sure," I say. "Set it up."

My dad taught me to play chess when I was seven because my mother didn't know how and he didn't have anyone else to play with. For four years, we played a game every night before I went to bed. That's how long it took before I finally beat him. He never let me win.

But now he gets tired halfway through the game. His eyes are starting to glaze over a little, and I spare his queen. He notices that I am helping him, that I am letting him win. He gets sad. And so do I.

Strategy #3: Accept Help.

A couple of moves later, I take his queen. I try and look satisfied and smug, but I don't feel it.

• • • •

I can still picture my father running up the stairs to break up a fight between me and my brother. Now he is huddled on the floor with blood droplets clinging to his hair.

One minute you're a baseball star, a draft candidate, running up the stairs; and the next you can't cross a room without losing your balance and spilling your head on the Formica. I pack the wheelchair into the trunk and try not to think of my father slow dancing on New Year's Eve, jumping up and down while he watches football, reaching things on the top shelf. I help him stumble to the car. It was my mother's birthday present six years ago, but it turns out she wanted the house instead. She got it, and we found a more accessible place for me and dad: wide doorways, low cabinets, high toilets, grab bars mounted on the walls. The license plate on the car still reads "DANS GRL." And since he can't drive anymore, the car went to me.

Dad's girl.

I try not to think about how my headrest is going to look crusted with dried blood and fallen hair. I pack the wheelchair into the trunk.

"It's like mom says," he says.

"What's that?"

"You have to put it all behind you. That's all over now. You just have to let it go."

He says that last part sort of sing songy and I try to remember the last time I cried about this.

Strategy #4: Sense of Humor.

It takes twenty-eight minutes to get to the hospital on a good day. This is the best multiple sclerosis research center in the country. My record is twenty. Today it takes twenty-seven. I drag the wheelchair out of the trunk and try desperately to attach the removable footrests without taking off my gloves. It is nine degrees outside. With the wind chill, it is negative seven. I pull my gloves off in disgust and secure the footrests.

In the waiting room it is easy to tell which people are waiting for appointments: they are stiff and shake, they walk awkwardly or slur their speech. It's always the same symptoms, the big ones anyway. First, part of your body goes numb. You ignore it or your wife tells you to ignore it. You push it back as long as you can. No one really wants to know when there's something wrong. Then, your vision starts to go in and out. Blind spots. Double vision. Right eye. Left eye. Camera one. Camera two. If you're really special, my dad's doctor explains, you'll lose your sense of taste, too. The doctors love these cases. You get extra MRIs, extra solumedral, acupuncture combined with small electric impulses, the whole deal only super-sized. The works. For thirty-nine cents they'll throw in a home steroid treatment twice a week. Upgrade. MS version 7.0.

When an inexplicable neurological disease starts to eat away at the brain myelin protecting your taste buds everything you eat tastes like Crisco oil. Warm Crisco oil with little Crisco bacon bits on top. Cold Crisco oil with seeds that get stuck in your teeth. Would you like your Crisco toasted? Salted? On a bun? With a fork? You could eat vomit, an orange peel, and a peanut butter sundae and it would all just taste like textured Crisco Oil. Such little roadblocks on the information super-highway of your spinal cord. A foolproof diet plan.

None of this is permanent right away. But eventually, it all is.

Then you can't balance. You can't walk. The ground is a funhouse mirror. Your legs feel twelve feet too long or three feet too short. You are always on a merry-go-round, an airplane, a bus that has to circle a parking lot at 54 miles per hour.

His hands are still shaking when we leave the hospital. My gloves are off to the remove the footrests, and on before I touch the steering wheel.

Once the car heats up enough, he tells me about the procedures. After she sealed up his head, the doctor gave him steroids to shrink his brain. This will pull the coiled gray stuff back from the lining of his skull and release the pressure on the nerves. But not for three or four more days. Brain shrinking is a delicate process.

Then they injected him with some cow myelin. Like throwing bread crusts to concentration camp victims. Let the disease chew on that for a while. Cows. People. My father. It doesn't really matter. Not to it. It just loves myelin.

He shivers and adjusts the bandage on his head.

I turn up the heat.

"Don't worry about me," he says, "it's just the steroids. It'll go away."

It's all permanent in the end, but I don't say that.

Strategy #5: Stay Positive.

The gloves come back off. The footrests go back on.

••••

My dad used to sing to me if I couldn't fall asleep and now he slurs his words so badly I can barely understand him.

And I know he's having trouble understanding me, too. It's the Nuerontin, the Dilantin, the Avonex. I feel the side effects right along with him these days. The Nausea, the Confusion, the Depression. It's amazing how some things seem to be contagious.

Strategy #6: Share with Others.

"You want to move out?" He says this calmly and slowly, but even so it takes me three times to understand.

There is no simple answer to this question. I think no, but

I don't say it. I think yes, but I don't say that either. I think, Mark got to pick where he went to college. I can sort of feel the tears starting back behind my eyes.

He says, "Of course I don't want to stop you. If that's what you want. I think journalism is perfect for you. But honey, New York? You've always been such a homebody."

Dad's girl.

I say, "Dad, I'll come home all the time. And we'll hire someone to help you or you could stay with Uncle Tim."

I think "nursing home," but I sure as hell don't say that. It's enough for him giving up golf, and fishing trips, his wife, his kids. His sense of normalcy. His body, the way he had gotten used to it.

"I don't want you to feel like you have to stay here. I don't want you to be chained down to me. I already feel like I've put too much strain on you. I know I ask a lot and it isn't fair."

He says something I can't understand and starts to cry a little.

"I want you to know I love just talking to you. It might not mean much to you, but it's important to me. And I know it's hard because we don't go out or play catch and I get so tired. But just because it's different doesn't mean it can't still be great."

At least, I think that's what he says.

I don't know where all my strength goes, but suddenly it's gone.

My father is not the sentimental type. He took me to Wendy's when I got my first period. He buys me men's shaving crème. He never wraps presents.

I can't handle him crying because I know it's me, and not the medicine.

So I start crying, too.

I tell him, "It's just if I get in. I'll call home everyday. I'll come home all the time."

But I'm not crying because my dad is sick. I'm not crying

because I know he'll never get any better. I am not crying because I miss my mother or Mark. And I'm not crying because I feel sad or guilty about leaving him. It's not because I think he'll feel abandoned or because I'm afraid of him being alone.

I'm crying because no matter what choice I make, the outcome is going to suck. For me, at least. Selfish moves like this come easy to the women in my family.

Strategy #7: Take Control

Strategy #8: Seize the Day.

Strategy #9: Decide That You Have MS, But That MS Doesn't Have You.

The voice of Mark in my head says, "Fucking lame."

••••

I spend the night at my mother's house where I still have a bedroom that hasn't been touched in months.

Strategy #10: Maintain Social Contacts.

The car looks right parked in this driveway again, but everything else about it feels wrong. I keep listening for the brakes on my dad's rolling walker. I pull out the folded corners of runners and throw rugs, so my dad won't trip over them, even though he isn't there. I push in chairs. I wonder how long it took my mother to stop thinking about these things.

At dinner we sit in our old places at the kitchen table.

My mother asks, "How's your father?"

There are empty chairs where Mark and my dad used to sit, and suddenly sitting diagonal from my mother feels strange.

She says, "I tried calling, a week ago, but I couldn't understand what he was saying. Is he slurring his speech again?"

I say, "I guess you already know."

She leaves the room and comes back with a file folder: manila, generic, like the one I keep brochures in at home. She takes a birthday card out it and hands it to me.

On the outside it says: "Happy Birthday," and there are still a few flakes of glitter clinging to a cartoon three-tier birthday cake.

I look at her, skeptically. It is not my birthday.

She says, "Your father gave me this."

On the inside, the message is covered up. I can see partial letters in printed blue ink, twelve point font, Brush Script MT. The picture taped over it is of my mom's car, my car, vanity plate shining.

"All my love, Dan." Even though it is six years old, I can tell his handwriting. My mind goes to the de-evolving signatures on the form for his safety deposit box. Sometimes I study them over his shoulder while he signs. 1990 to 1995 they are almost all the same. Then 96 was a bad year. Better in 97, and a steady decline since 2000.

"Your father was just starting to get bad that year," she says. "He started walking with a cane, then the walker."

"I know," I say. "Now we don't leave the house without the wheelchair."

She nods, slowly, choosing her words carefully. "I was upset that we couldn't take walks anymore, like we used to. He would get so tired. Then he went on disability. I had to work twice as hard."

"I know," I say again. "I was there."

"There was no time for us to be a couple. It's better this way. It's better now that we have time to talk, and we don't yell."

She backs off for the rest of the night, giving me time to think and stare at my homework. In between, I study my father's words on the card. The open loops in "All my love." And in clear, careful printing on the back of the photo: "If we didn't have time for a walk. I'd take you for a ride."

My mother kisses me good-bye the next morning saying, "Sometimes people have to find new ways to love each other."

••••

I get a letter from NYU.

My dad's been doing a little bit better. His vision's cleared up and his speech is almost normal. He took a cab to his doctor's appointment so I didn't have to miss school. But nothing's ever really "better." It's always some symptoms go away, some new ones appear. And every time you have to wonder, will this be the time it doesn't go away?

I've been a little better, too. I turned down a chess game last month, for the first time since my dad got sick. I'm feeling more like his daughter again, rather than his nurse. So when my letter comes, I actually get excited. But, I don't tell my dad yet. I decide not to open it until after dinner.

At dinner I ask, "How was your appointment?"

"Fine," he says.

He always says fine, so you have to learn how to gauge it for yourself. Today he seems a little hesitant.

"What happened?"

"Nothing really," he says, weakly, "you know that pain I've been having in my jaw?"

I nod. He describes it like biting on a pin when his mouth opens and closes. The doctor's been doubling his Dilantin every week.

"Sure," I say. "More Dilantin?"

He says, "No. The doctor wants to do a small surgery and clip the nerve. She said it should stop the pain entirely. It's about 85% effective."

"Jaw surgery?"

He says, "Well, no. They have to cut it at the base of the brain."

"Brain surgery?" I ask.

He says, "She thinks it's the best option. She thinks we might as well try it, rather than just wait it out."

Strategy #11: Be Proactive.

I nod. This will be his second brain surgery, and the idea of it makes me feel awful. Everyone at the hospital talks to you like you're made out of glass. They give you a pager and tell you to wait. They make you bring a will. They assure you: it is just in case.

"When?"

"Soon. As soon as she can clear an appointment time. Maybe Friday."

I nod again and finish eating. I try to pretend it doesn't bother me, because it doesn't seem to bother him. Maybe because he's not the one in the waiting room, watching the pager for a little red light, holding a photocopy of his father's will. When I am finished, I excuse myself.

I tell him I am going to read.

"Hun?" He says. "Don't worry about it. Think of this way, at least it means a lot less Dilantin."

He draws circles around his ears with his index fingers, trying to show how the medicine makes him crazy. I don't think it's very funny, but I smile anyway.

I am thinking about my mother when I open my letter from the journalism program at NYU. I wonder if she sometimes wishes she could love him as her husband again.

I read the first line and it's enough for me.

The letter says, "We would like to congratulate you…"

The brochure says, "It is important to make decisions that are the best for your own life. Your family member with MS will support you and help you make the right decision."

My dad's voice in my head says, "Go."

Outside my window, it is warming up. It is good driving weather and my mom's car, my car, in the driveway looks lonely and ready.

Certainty
· · · · · · · · · · · ·

Right from the start, Cris was pretty certain she could get me pregnant. It started on our honeymoon—a six day trip to Vegas where we stayed at the Venetian, ate at the Paris and drank all night at New York, New York. We took a gondola ride to the elevators and made out like high school kids. In our room, Cris slid her soft hands under my cotton skirt. She rubbed against me, her leg between my legs.

"Let's make a baby," she whispered.

My breathless laugh came out like a moan. "What?" I asked.

"Let's make a baby," she said again. "Right now. To-night."

She rubbed her cheek against my cheek and I played along. "Okay," I said. "Knock me up."

When we were finished, she put her hand on my abdomen, traced a ring around my belly button.

"Do you think we did it?"

I turned to look at her. Her eyes were wide and hopeful. "Are you joking?" I asked. "You know you can't actually get me pregnant."

"How do you know that?"

"Because I took a biology class. In third grade."

"Sometimes unexpected things happen," she said.

"Not like this."

I had come to terms with the fact that I would never be able to have a baby with the person I loved a long time ago. Sometimes I went to chat rooms for infertile women and read a month's worth of posts in one sitting. I cried and cried. I knew exactly how they felt. But it seemed Cris hadn't made peace with it. She brought it up again, when we were back at home in Ohio.

"I'm serious about wanting a baby, you know."

We were making dinner in our tiny kitchen. Cris was cleaning vegetables and I was trimming the fat from a couple of chicken breasts.

"I know," I said. "I want one, too."

"No, I mean, like, naturally."

"Cris, this freaks me out. That obviously can't happen."

"Why not?"

"We are both women."

"My aunt's doctor told her with 100% certainty she would never be able to have kids. He said her ovaries didn't function right and they never would and she should just forget it. They would have to try something else. Five years later, they adopted a little boy, and the next month they found out she was pregnant."

"What's your point?"

"Miracles happen. Miracles like that happen all the time."

She brought the peeler over the smooth surface of a potato.

She was so gentle, even when she was upset. I wanted to hold her from behind, press her hips against the metal sink, but my hands were covered in chicken juice.

"That's great for your aunt, Cris, but that won't happen for us. Neither of us has any sperm."

"But she had a zero percent chance, too. Same as us, and it happened because they love each other. And we love each other."

"Cris, you have to stop this. It's making me too sad. I cannot give you this. We will have children, I promise. But we have to do it another way."

"I want to do it this way."

"Didn't you let this go when you realized you were gay?"

"I thought I did," she said. She turned a potato over in her hand. "I guess I just didn't think I would love anyone this much."

Soon, it was all I could think about. And it was breaking my heart. If Cris and I could have a child together, I knew that kid would be the best, most interesting kid on the planet. But I also knew we couldn't. Every time we made love, Cris looked at me with this intense longing. She was trying to make it happen. I could tell. And sometimes, right before I came, I almost thought it was possible, too.

On Thursday, Cris came home from the grocery store with fresh tulips and a home pregnancy test.

"Just take it," she said.

"I'm not going to take it. It's humiliating."

"Why?"

"Because I'm not pregnant. And I just don't want to feel like I failed you or something."

"Then you think I'm failing."

"No, I don't. This is like asking a fish to grow feathers. I know you love me. I love you. I just don't think it's possible."

In the end, I took the test. I waited until Cris was out and unwrapped the layers of packaging like a Christmas gift. Unlike the women on the infertility boards, I had never taken a pregnancy test before. Maybe I just wanted to know what it would feel like. I set the timer on my cell phone. In three minutes it would all be over.

I watched my reflection in the bathroom mirror while the timer counted down. I suddenly felt nervous. I don't know why; I already knew what the test would say. But while I stood there, watching the empty gray box for any signs of change, I realized I did not know.

Hydrogen Event in a Bubble Chamber
●●

In the dream, I give birth in reverse. A man I don't recognize gets younger and smaller. I try to stop him, hold him up and keep him tall, but his adult body collapses into that of an infant in my waiting arms. Then, before I can establish even his eye color, he is vacuumed into my belly, where he makes me swell, then shrink, until I feel nothing but surprise. I lift my eyes. All around me people are shrinking, as if warped by too much gravity, and then getting pulled up into different women.

In the morning, over breakfast, I think, maybe, we've got this all wrong. What if things are really supposed to happen that way, and we should all be compacted and pulled into our mothers, and they into their mothers, and they into theirs; until, crushed to the size of a single infant, we are sucked into the overwhelming gravity of that first mother. And our first father stands by helplessly as a cord sprouts from his stomach and he doubles over, resigned, and starts to shrink.

I tell Marvin about my dream, even though we've just met, because his paper is on black holes and I think he might be interested. He acts like he is, even if he's not. Our tables are next to each other at the university's physics conference. All of the booths are manned by graduate students pursuing their degrees and showing off parts of their research. It is easy to tell the first years from the second years. The second years are already into their Ph.D. programs. Their displays are black and white diagrams on typing paper, or else nothing. Marvin and I, like the other first years, have tri-fold presentation boards decorated with household items painted to look like neutrinos or the electromagnetic field. None of the seven patrons have stopped by our booths yet. We chat out of boredom, but after a while I find him genuinely interesting.

Though we are in the same program at neighboring universities, we study with different professors and have radically different concentrations. Mine is supersymmetric string theory and its products, especially how it is able to interact with quantum physics on a sub-atomic level. Marvin tells me his is special relativity, the new visualization of gravity. My conference paper is on particles with half-integer spins and how M-theory manages to account for their exchange. It is a relatively new field, still largely theoretical, pioneered in the 1980s. It is the rock and roll of physics to his classical Mozart. I have an appreciation for the beauty, balance and stability of his equations that I'm not sure he has for the innovation, creativity and danger of mine, whose consequences have yet to be explored.

Marvin is tall, even sitting down, with thick wrists and a thick waist. His whole silhouette is soft. When he wraps his hand around his water glass his fingers widen and he has to spread them out a little. My fingers are long and thin. I have knobby joints like ball-bearings at each wrist. I could completely disappear behind Marvin. It is a feeling I'm not sure I like.

"Your dream may not be that far off," he tells me. "Studies have shown that the human brain makes no interesting distinctions between the past and the present. If someone looks at a hot dog, or remembers looking at the hot dog, the same parts of their brain light up."

I already know this. It has always made me wonder if consciousness is selective. If we only remember things the way we do because it's more attractive. We like to think of ourselves, of our minds, of our universe as expanding. But if there is no difference between what *is* happening and what *was* happening in our brains, is it possible we've only created this reality? That what we think of as experience, is only us remembering?

I ask Marvin, who shrugs and doesn't look at all convinced. He tells me he likes math, equations and experiments.

He says, "You're talking philosophy."

His exact words are: "If you can't test it, it's philosophy."

Two thousand years ago the shape of the earth was philosophy, I tell him. Maybe I'm ahead of my time.

Marvin starts to nod before I finish my sentence. "I knew you would say something like that."

••••

Our third date happens to be on my birthday. Marvin brings a present over when he comes to pick me up. It is wrapped, well even. There doesn't appear to be a card.

"Wow. Thanks," I say. "You didn't have to do this."

He says, "It's your birthday. This is what people do."

"I know," I say, "but you haven't known me that long. It's just bad luck my birthday's so soon."

"Are you trying to say I can't pick out a good present? I think I did quite well."

I smile. "Let's find out."

The package is big—flat, but looks almost two feet by a foot and a half—and heavy. I sit down to open it. Marvin helps. Inside is a picture, a print, professionally framed. The print is blue with curving white lines and little dots all over it.

"What is it?" I ask.

"It's a picture of subatomic particles, through an electron microscope. The technical term is 'hydrogen event in a bubble chamber.' It's what happens when two particles are smashed together at very high speeds. This one's from the accelerator at FermiLab. The lines and spots are tracks made by the explosion." He runs a bulky fingertip along one of the swirls. "See?"

I nod. "I really like it," I say. And I do. It reminds me of an old map, or an astrological chart. The circles are so perfect they look compass-drawn. "I can't believe this symmetry just happens. Doesn't it amaze you?"

Marvin shrugs. "You know, they can pretty much predict all this stuff now. If you know the size of the particles, their spin and how fast they're moving, you can calculate the force with which they'll hit and plot out how the pieces will move, and where they'll all end up. Theoretically, they could do it for anything, like an egg rolling off a table, or a car accident "

"If you had a fast enough computer," I say. "One that wouldn't overheat under the stress of running all those equations."

"Sure. But if we *did*, we could even plot out people's lives."

I want to ask if he means free will doesn't factor in at all, but I'm afraid of what he'll say.

I turn the picture over. There is an envelope, taped to the cardboard, with my name on it. The script looks choppy and uneven compared to the elegant shapes on the other side.

"You don't have to read that now," Marvin says. "It just says 'Happy Birthday' and other boring stuff like that. It's very generic. It would embarrass me."

"Let's hang the picture up," I say, already moving to the junk drawer for a nail.

"You have a hammer?" he asks.

I detect skepticism.

I pull a small tool case from the hall closet. It's pink and says "Ladies' Tools" on the side, embossed in fake cursive handwriting.

Marvin laughs.

I open it and remove a pink-handled hammer from among the pink wrench, pink measuring tape, pink screwdriver.

"My dad gave me these when I moved out to go to college. They were very popular in my dorm," I say in my defense.

I hand him the hammer. It looks miniature in his big hand, like a toy for a little girl.

••••

Marvin comes over and we drink red wine on my small back porch. It is cool outside and he lets me sit on his lap. We share a blanket, a twin sized fleece throw. It is too short to wrap around ourselves, so we drape it over both of us. The backs of my legs are cold from the breeze coming under the chair. I try to line my legs up with his for warmth, to block the wind, but I can't balance. It's okay, though. I prefer cold ankles to the thought of being away from him, even a short distance, even for a moment. We look at the moon even though we both know it is only reflective rock and dust. We don't stare at it because of its mystery, but because it is pretty for what it is.

Marvin tells me that someday a small black hole orbiting the earth will power our entire planet.

I disagree. "Even if it were possible to harness that energy," I say, "The nearest one is light years away. We could never have one close enough to orbit."

Marvin shakes his head. "We could move them. They have incredibly powerful gravitational pulls."

He's right, of course, in theory. You could dangle a piece of matter in front of it, like a large meteor or a small planet. If you keep it far enough away from the event horizon that it doesn't get sucked in, the black hole will just follow it. Like a carrot in front of a donkey.

This makes me think about how folklore and tradition might be different if the Earth had a black hole instead of a moon. Maybe our fascination for things that shine would be shifted to things that attract. I imagine Romeo and Juliet discussing magnets instead of moonbeams. The division of the year into "months" would be a product of menstruation instead of the waxing and waning of a glowing orb. Women would carry with us, each, our own black hole. A source of life and energy. A mysterious place: small, but with infinite draw.

Marvin and I make love on the porch, him on his back on the thin fleece throw, me on top with most of my clothes still on. He leaves some of himself inside me. It has been swallowed, pulled past the event horizon where it will be absorbed forever. He will never get that back, that part of himself. I love how I don't have to give him anything. I leave whole. I leave stronger.

Afterward, his sweat starts to chill us both and we dress quickly in the cold. The wine is gone and we move inside, holding hands. I wonder if Marvin thinks I'm going to tell him that I love him. He puts his arms under my ribcage and squeezes.

He whispers, "You need to get some bug spray."

But there are no bugs. I tell him.

"In May," he says, "there will be."

Marvin shakes the dust off the blanket, bull-fighter style. I think about his bug spray comment. I wonder if this means he plans to be with me, making love on my back porch, in May.

Or if he is just genuinely concerned that I might get mosquito bites. Either way, I think, it is a good sign.

••••

Cohomology dictates that the fabric of our universe can't change shape. It can bend and shift, expand and contract, but it cannot tear where there are no tears, or heal itself where there are. So, a basketball could be reshaped into a brick or a table, but not a coffee mug or a doughnut. A doughnut can be a record or a paper towel roll, but not a pair of scissors, and so on. This cohomology is essentially the only thing that allows for difference. On the scale of about a Planck length, this is the only insurmountable obstacle in changing matter. I find it odd that human gender would be separated by so great a barrier. I am a coffee cup. As much as I may love, or feel a sense of belonging with a brick, we will never be alike in this most basic sense. I will always be more complicated, more elegantly composed and more versatile. This discovery comes with a sense of entitlement, and frustration.

I tell Marvin this idea at dinner.

He is familiar with cohomology, he says, but he doesn't think it applies.

I try to explain again.

We have been together two months and are celebrating. This is also the first time I've seen him in almost a week. Dr. Conn has him at the library fifty hours a week researching spin vectors of hypothetical particles. Marvin starts to glaze over about the time I get to the coffee cup again.

"Yeah," he says, "I get it. But I don't think you're right. I don't think you can apply it on such a large scale. Anyway, if it's that important to you, if you feel like I need to be a coffee cup for us to connect, I'll just get my ear pierced or something."

His comment stings, but I shrug it off. "I just think it's interesting."

We drive to my apartment in silence. Twenty miles over the speed limit, the way the stars look like world lines is the same way my contacts drying on my eyes makes the streetlamps look like light cones. The reflection in my darkened window makes it look like Marvin is running beside the car. I keep passing him by. And he keeps coming back.

••••

If we could visualize life in four dimensions, we could plot a world line for every existing thing. Instead of only locating a specific object or person at a point in three spatial dimensions, we could drag its position point into the fourth dimension of space-time. So, the world line of a bird would trace its entire history through all its different points in space and through all time. It would be as if there were a million birds of different sizes, one for every instant of its life, at a different point. But they would be attached, like paper dolls, or the stretchy blur of color you get when you take a picture of something in motion. The bird then, though small in our perceivable three dimensions, would be expansive.

Normally I love this idea because it makes me feel bigger than I am, like I can change my shape based on where I move. But today, it makes me sad. I've spent the last three days on my porch moving between the folding chair and the side railing, where I've balanced a bottle of Orange-glo to kill bees with. If you traced my world line, I would still be small. Smaller than Marvin. Smaller than this porch. And mostly, you would only see the still image of me in the folding chair, chin balanced perfectly on my left fist. This image would be clear, like a picture and uninteresting, like a stone.

I haven't seen Marvin for fifteen days. He's found a correlation while tabling Dr. Conn's particles and wants to look into it as something that might turn into his master's thesis. It wasn't until day nine that I started to think he didn't miss me. And not until day twelve that I knew it. I call Marvin and ask him to come over. He barely hesitates before saying yes. He must already know he won't be over for long. He must already know what I am going to say.

When I open the door he looks excited, even flushed. I think he might rush to me, pressing his soft belly against mine. Instead he moves past me without any contact, which is not an easy feat in my narrow hallway. He finds a pen on my desk and starts scratching notes into his palm.

"I thought of something on the way over. A new way to organize."

Seeing him again, I want to touch him. But I am resolved. I will wait for him to come to me. I tell myself, I'll give him twenty seconds. Ten. Five.

Finally, he puts his eyes, but not his hands on me. "Right," he says, "you wanted to talk."

"Marvin," I say, "I'm exhausted waiting for you. I can't understand why you don't love me, or love life, the way you love physics. "

He tells me, "Life is physics."

But it's not. His elegant equations can't explain why I've spent the last three days on my tiny back porch. And why, surrounded by pine trees, I can't smell anything but the orange-glo I tried to kill the bugs with.

It can't even explain why I don't remember what happens to us tomorrow.

Marvin smiles. For a second I think it might be a break-through; but, I know, it doesn't fit the pattern.

He says, "I told you to buy bug spray."

And it all comes together. I love him for his creativity and brilliance, because being with him is like always having a new CD by my favorite artist: comfortable, but surprising and moving in a fresh, but expected way. Because he is smarter than I am.

He loves me because I am always me. He knows my composition, sure as rock, and doesn't love me because there is mystery, but because I am pretty for what I am. Like a formula, he knew what to put in and with the right amount of thought, what would come out. And like listening to his favorite song, he must have always known how it would end: the drum fill, the high note, cool summer tears, the smell of Orange-glo. But even so, he wanted to get here.

There is mystery in that for me, and comfort.

"I need more than this," I say. "I need more than the occasional dinner together and advice about pesticides."

"I know," he says.

"I need to feel like I'm affecting something."

He nods. He's making eye contact, but I can feel him trying not to look down at the numbers on his palm. After a while, he leaves.

I look at the print he'd had framed for me: its deep blue background, its swirling calligraphy like skate tracks on a frozen pond. I look at it until I don't want to see it anymore. I take it down, lifting it from its nail in one swift motion. Without it, the whole room looks different, empty.

Marvin's envelope is still taped to the back. I'd forgotten about it when he hung the picture. I spend some time thinking about putting it in the shoebox where I keep old letters, or throwing it away, or sending it back. But I don't think of opening it. Of running my fingertip along the seal. Of looking for the thin, transparent half-moons of dried paper where his tongue slipped off, just for a second.

I don't think about that. Not even for a second.

The Snakeskin

·················

Mr. Adleman calls an assembly because he thinks it is some kind of prank. At nine a.m. in the big gym, he holds it up for everyone to see. It is a snakeskin, clearly. Even the students in the top row of the bleachers can see that. Even the ones with eyeglasses. Even the ones with borderline myopia who don't wear their eyeglasses because they don't like the way they look in them can see what it is.

The snakeskin is huge, as snakeskins go. It is at least four feet long. The students see the pattern of scales running across its back. They see its slow taper into the tail. There is a tattered opening where the head should be, but other than that it is in one exquisite piece. Both fluid and stiff, it waves a bit when Mr. Adleman gestures. It flops around beneath his hand as he says, "...not funny" and "...consequences of this behavior." He vows to find the students responsible for bringing the snakeskin into his school and punish them severely.

The thing is, though, a month goes by and nothing is found out. No one claims responsibility. Mr. Adleman becomes increasingly frustrated. He calls another assembly in which he encourages students to do their own detective work. He says, "I know you all probably already know who did this. Your silence isn't helping anyone." The students look around at each other. Mr. Adleman offers a pair of free prom tickets to any student who comes forward with information about the snakeskin.

Another month goes by and no information has come to light. There are meetings with Mr. Adleman, six students at a time, in which the students swear they haven't heard anyone take credit for the snakeskin being in their school. Mr. Adleman threatens to cancel the prom if no one speaks up, but no one does. The students begin to walk around nervously. The weather is turning warmer, but the girls forgo their strappy footwear in favor of closed sneakers. Female teachers switch to pants. Everyone wears socks, even the art teacher who sports a thick woolen pair under her Birkenstocks. "If you think about it," the students say, "that can't even be the size of the snake now. He was too *big* for that skin."

In April, teachers find four more skins. They are smaller, but the scale patterns indicate that this is the same kind of snake. Mr. Adleman stops calling assemblies. He cancels interrogations. Students pile their schoolbooks under the legs of their desks to raise them off the ground. They stalk through the hallways with their eyes glued to the tile floor. The girls stick their feet straight out in front of them when they use the bathroom. Many students claim to have seen a snake, but the descriptions are varied and largely discredited by the majority of the students. Still, parents begin writing notes to accompany their children's dress code violations: "Due to the snakes, please allow Jeremy to wear his steel-toed boots during gym class."

Senior prom is held in the big gym, which is transformed by balloons and colored lights. The students walk through a curtain of metallic streamers. Many of the girls shiver as the streamers rub their bare shoulders. The boys on the soccer team wear their shin guards over their tuxedos. The girls wear tennis shoes and leggings under their formal dresses. In the real couples, the ones whose romance will last well into June, the boys carry the girls in front of them like infants. But still, no one is relaxed. No one is having fun. Several students request the lights be turned up. In the end, they all climb up onto the bleachers and watch the floor. Periodically, someone jumps up and points to the painted foul line or rounded three-point line in fear. Then everyone laughs nervously.

At the end of the night, the students ask Mr. Adleman to take down the streamers. He climbs onto a chair and peels the tape from above the doorframe. The students file out silently. Long after they are gone, Mr. Adleman stays on the chair in the dark gym watching the floor.

Advice for Dealing with the Loss of a Beloved Pet

••

1. Pay attention to your feelings.

The Holts find out about Ethan's cancer three weeks after they find out about Millie's. The vet points it out to Ethan, who is there to talk about Millie's prognosis.

"She has appendicular osteosarcoma, bone cancer. It seems to be localized to her back left leg."

"What should we do?" Ethan asks.

"The cancer is treatable. We would have to remove the tumor to stop the pain. In Millie's case, we'd probably need to remove most of the leg. Then she'd have a course of chemotherapy to keep other cancer cells contained."

"Will that cure her?"

Dr. Linken shrugs. "It would give her two years, probably. Maybe three. Many pet owners choose to end their pets' pain without the surgery." He waits to make sure Ethan understands. He does. "It's an option."

Ethan is rehearsing what he will say to his wife, Claire, when the vet interrupts his thoughts.

"Have you had that lump on your throat looked at?"

"This?" asks Ethan, touching the fleshy bump right below his Adam's apple. He thought it was a swollen lymph node from a fading cold.

The vet rubs Ethan's throat. "Swallow," he commands. "Have you been feeling anxious lately? Having trouble sleeping? Losing weight?"

Ethan nods after each question. There is a simple explanation; he's worried about Millie. She's been limping around the house, barely eating anything, licking her stiff leg.

"I think you've got a nodule on your thyroid gland there. We see it all the time in cats. Go get it looked at. I'd check it myself, but our scanner doesn't even fit Great Danes."

Ethan senses that he is supposed to laugh.

"It's probably nothing," the vet says.

2. Accept the reality of what has happened.

It turns out it isn't nothing; it is papillary thyroid cancer. Ethan sits in the oncologist's office, petting the bump, while Dr. Francis explains the treatment to Claire. There will be a surgery to remove the affected lobe of his thyroid gland, then chemotherapy with radioactive iodine to kill the remaining cancer cells. The prognosis is good. They've caught it early. No cervical bone involvement, no affected lymph nodes. The doctor asks them if they have any questions. Ethan is sure he has thousands, but he can't think of a single one.

At home, Claire adds Ethan's surgery date to their wall

calendar with a thick blue marker. She makes dinner, which they eat in silence. Ethan can feel the tumor moving up and down under his skin as he swallows small bites of salmon.

"We should talk about Millie," he says. They haven't talked about her since the vet's visit almost two weeks ago. Once the center of Claire's life like a furry, four-legged daughter, it's amazing how quickly Millie faded out of her field of vision.

"Really, Ethan? You want to talk about that now?"

"Is there ever going to be a good time? She's in pain, Claire. Don't you think we should do something?"

Claire looks in the direction of Millie's pet bed, hidden by the kitchen's south wall and its cheery custard wallpaper.

Ethan goes on. "I think we should put her down. It's the right thing to do."

"No!" Claire exclaims, immediately in tears. "We're not just going to kill her because she's sick. We'll do the amputation. We'll help her get better."

"Claire, we can't put a dog through that kind of torture. Wouldn't it be better if Millie never had to feel any pain ever again?"

"We can fight this with her. I don't want to lose her. Not now."

"We need to think about what's best for Millie."

"You think it's best for her to die, Ethan? Just because she's sick? Don't you think being alive is worth a little pain?"

Ethan pushes rice around on his plate. They are no longer talking about Millie. Ethan isn't sure Claire can keep these two things separate. "Of course, Claire," he says. "We'll do the treatment. We'll call Dr. Linken tomorrow."

3. Talk to someone who has been through it.

They schedule Millie's surgery for two days after Ethan's. She'll stay at the animal hospital for forty-eight hours and they can focus on Ethan's recovery until he's strong enough to walk around.

Both surgeries go well. The surgeons remove the right lobe of Ethan's thyroid gland without any damage to the parathyroid glands or the laryngitic nerve. The veterinary technicians remove Millie's left hind leg at the joint. Dr. Linken is confident the cancer hasn't spread to Millie's hips.

For two weeks Millie and Ethan rest, eat what they can and swallow pain killers every four hours on the button. Ethan wears a foam neck brace to keep his neck immobilized while his stitches heal. Millie wears a plastic cone around her neck to keep her from chewing on her bandage. Ethan walks around the house like Frankenstein's monster, turning his shoulders when he needs to turn his head. He watches Millie bump her giant cone against the lip of her water dish.

"What do you think, little girl? Does it feel like you're missing something?" he says, his voice still strangled from the surgery. He stoops to pet her awkwardly, unable to look down into her eyes.

But Millie does seem to be in less pain. She is already walking just fine; she'd probably gotten used to walking without putting any weight on her sore back leg. Her appetite has increased. She is friendlier, happier. Her improvements rub off on Claire who, after spending weeks dragging herself around the house as if in shackles, now flits from the kitchen to the living room like a hummingbird.

"Everything I've read says the surgery is the hardest part," she says. "The chemo for thyroid cancer is the easiest chemo there is. The thyroid is the only thing that uses iodine, so the rest of your body isn't even affected. No hair loss, no weight loss."

"No hair loss! Good thing!" Ethan says, touching his receding hairline.

Claire laughs and the sound of her laughter surprises him. It has been a while since he's heard it.

4. Don't isolate yourself.

Ethan's chemotherapy takes place one month after his surgery. The radioactive iodine they dose him with will concentrate in his thyroid gland, killing it and any remaining cancer cells. For one week, Ethan has to isolate himself completely. The radioactive iodine in his body could harm anyone he comes in contact with. After seven days, the iodine will no longer be radioactive and he can go home to Claire and Millie and this whole thing will be over. Ethan books a hotel room for the week following his treatment.

Claire thinks it is the perfect time for Millie to have her treatment as well. She'll likely be nauseous and lethargic. Someone will have to puree wet dog food with plain rice for Millie to eat. Someone will have to squirt water into her mouth with a squeeze bottle if she's too weak to reach her water bowl. Someone will have to clean up after her.

"I'll do it while you're gone," Claire says. "It'll be easiest. I can focus all my attention on Millie."

"Why don't you wait until I'm back," Ethan asks. His scar smiles at Claire, then frowns, then smiles again as his Adam's apple jogs up and down. "I can help you."

"It's better like this," she says. "I promise. It'll give me something to focus on so I don't have to worry about you."

Reluctantly, Ethan consents.

"This is almost over," Claire says. "We're so close."

During his isolation, Ethan thinks about Millie. The iodine doesn't make him sick, Claire is right about that. But as his thyroid slowly dies, it dumps massive amounts of hormone into his blood stream. This makes him sicker than he has ever been. On the hotel bed he sweats and shakes. He vomits until both trashcans are full, then drags them to the bathroom to empty them. When he can muster the strength, he rinses them before placing them back on the bed and climbing in beside them. Housekeeping knocks on his door over and over again. No one can come in. When he calls Claire, she tells him Millie is doing all right. A little sickness, not too bad.

"How are you?" she asks.

"I'm just fine," he says. He doesn't want to worry her. He suspects she's playing the same game with her reports on Millie. "I'm looking forward to being back home," he says. "With my girls."

5. Write about your feelings.

There are bills in the mail almost every day. First from Memorial, where Ethan had his surgery, then from St. Bonaventure Animal Hospital. $170 for x-rays. $220 for a surgery consultation. $125 for a nuclear scan. $270 for chemotherapy. $540 for chemotherapy. When the bills are in piles, outside of their envelopes, Ethan has trouble determining whose are whose.

He writes check after check. He puts "chemo" in the memo line, or "drugs," or "test," or "Millie." He can't remember the last time he wrote something that wasn't a check. It is a lot of money to spend on an extra year or two for Millie. He tries not to think about how much money they've spent on him, or how long it may have bought him. He supposes it is good that they never had children.

There are two more tests: full body scans for Ethan and Millie to make sure the cancers are really gone. Ethan's costs $90 out of pocket. Millie's is $190. All these years they laughed at their crazy friends who bought pet insurance. It's the accountants in the animal hospital who are laughing now.

Ethan convinces Claire that he and Millie should have their scans on the same day.

"I can drive myself," he insists. "It'll just make me worried if you're there with me. It's going to be fine. Remember how early they caught it?"

"You'll call me the second you know anything?"

"Yes. And we'll meet up back at home and celebrate. All the Holts will officially be in remission."

Ethan lies as still as possible in the scanner. He thinks about how Millie is the only person who knows how he's feeling, and Millie isn't even a person—she's a dog.

"Please lie still, Mr. Holt," the technician says. "We're almost done."

We're almost done. He repeats it to himself. *We're almost done.*

6. Prepare a memorial for your pet.

Ethan's scan is clean as a whistle. He picks up steaks on the way home from the hospital. One for him, one for Claire and one for Millie. She deserves it, the old girl. He knows exactly what she's been through and it isn't pretty.

He is putting the steaks into a hot pan when Claire comes home from the vet.

"How's our girl?" he shouts over the sizzling oil.

Claire comes into the kitchen. Her eyes are red.

"Claire, everything's fine," he says. "I'm good as new. Where's Millie?"

She turns off the burner, leads him to the couch, sits down beside him. "It was in her lungs, Ethan."

Ethan is still looking around for Millie. He sees her leash on the dining room table. Her collar is there, too. "What did you do?" he asks.

"She couldn't take anymore, Ethan. You didn't see her when she had the chemo. She was so…." Claire's voice catches in her throat. "It was awful."

"I know it's awful. I was sick as a fucking dog that week." He hears the pun as he is saying it. "Shit. You know what I mean."

60

"There was nothing else we could do. Dr. Linken agreed. It's like you said, why torture her?"

"Like I said? What the hell do you mean? Is she gone?" Ethan is sweating. He can feel his skin turning red. "You put her down? Without me there?" The knot in his throat is unbelievably painful. He can feel every stitch. Every dead cell. "I thought we were in this together."

"We are, Ethan. I'm right here."

But he doesn't mean Claire, he means Millie. He knows, even through his despair, that Claire is right. The treatment gave Millie a little more time. When Millie got better, it gave him hope. Sometime soon he will feel grateful for that. But now all he feels is pain and the gaps left behind by all the missing pieces.

Made in Indonesia

My coffee is cold because I'm too involved in my book to touch it. And then there is fresh chai tea on the table next to me.

This is how I meet Sam.

For a long time we've been going to the same coffee shop to read. It's one of those artsy places where they serve free trade coffee and soy milk in hand-made ceramic pottery. There is new-age experimental art on the walls. The napkins are recycled from when you were there two months ago and all the tablecloths are from thrift stores.

The patrons resemble the shop. They've recycled their personalities from the people they had coffee with two months ago, so nothing ever seems consistent.

Like the vegetarian who always wears Nikes. Save the animals. Oppress the humans.

One of the paintings on the wall is mine, but no one's bought it yet. It's too traditional, I guess. It is oil paint on a black background. Deep blues and intense purples. The picture is of a girl huddled inside the hollow of a dead tree. A pencil is balanced on a near limb. The pencil is blue, too.

Contrast this with the other art:

The giant-sized blow-ups of Superman's nose hairs.

The magazine collages of Bill Clinton jerking off.

The splatter-paint therapy sessions.

The boy who brought me chai tea says: "I've seen you here before."

I hate chai tea, I say.

"We have that in common," he says and sits down to share his hot chocolate.

••••

A month later we're feeling each other out over hot apple cider.

The guy at the counter with spray-in green hair is always staring at me. Sam hates it.

We're each trying to decide, who is more involved? Who stands to lose the most? What are my odds? I keep a straight face when they show celebrity weddings on the six o'clock news.

Someone is ordering a latte, insisting on soy. His belt is leather.

My painting is still on the wall and there's a layer of dust collecting along the top of the frame. Sam hates it.

He says: "It doesn't speak to me."

Of course it doesn't, it's a painting. But I don't say that. I tell him I must just see something he doesn't see.

"It's not the worst piece in here," he says. He gestures to

his cup, which is way too thick on one side. You can see the finger indentations from whoever lovingly sculpted it. What a piece of crap.

He is comparing my art to someone's attempt at functionality. I wonder how long this can last.

••••

Then it's been five months and we are annoying the hell out of each other. His idea of a romantic gesture is buying condoms that are ribbed for my pleasure. I don't even show him my paintings anymore.

I order a chai tea because I am feeling nostalgic, but I don't like it. Sam calls my cell phone from a party, tells me I should meet him. There are a lot of people here, he says. The pot is A-plus. And am I mad at him?

I'm not mad. I just hate feeling alone when I am not alone. I have to go, I say.

As it is, I have to scream. A group of lesbians are shouting lines from Julius Caesar between sips of espresso. Everyone is wearing togas, even the director. The girl playing Brutus has been at all the same protests as me, but she works at the Gap.

I look at my painting and realize it's been there so long that the wallpaper is probably darker underneath it. Suddenly Sam is infinite distances away.

••••

It's been almost a year and I've developed a taste for chai tea.

"You're breaking up with me?" Sam says.

I hate that he says it like that. I'm not breaking anything. I'm not putting a baseball bat to the time we've spent together. I'm not taking the way his pillow smells and backing over it with my car. Everything will be intact, just stopped. I need to put everything on hold.

64

I'm just putting you on hold, I say.

That all sounded better in my head.

"This sucks," he says.

No kidding, I say.

What is this, a movie? I say.

You have to narrate? I say.

He doesn't even justify it with a response.

"Can I ask why?"

There are a thousand reasons and then there are none. I can't think of where to begin and then I can't think of anything at all. The tag on the tablecloth is rubbing against my leg. I grab it. Made in Indonesia. I roll my eyes.

He doesn't look at me the way he did when we first met. I haven't been surprised in months. I don't say any of this.

I say, I dunno.

He looks like he might cry and I try my best to look like that. But I don't feel it. This was re-sale love. The sleeves are too short or the pants are ripped at one seam. I get lost in my own metaphors.

••••

I stayed away from the coffee shop for a little while. I guess I got sick of those Abercrombie and Fitch types who buy clothes at full price that are faded to look like they came from thrift stores. Plus, I heard a rumor that they don't use free trade coffee after all. But of course I missed it. Everything, I mean.

So I go back and nothing's changed. The head of our recycling committee is throwing his plastic juice bottle in the trash.

The owner walks up to me and drops thirty dollars on the table.

"Someone bought your picture," he says.

I get excited for a minute before I ask. Who?

"That lady who has a new palm pilot every week and never tips."

Oh, I say. It wasn't Sam. And it didn't even leave a dark spot on the wall.

It's like it was never there.

The Specialists
·················

By the end of our first day of basic, word was out that Jakewad had raped a girl once and gotten away with it. He
didn't brag about it or anything; it was Net that spread the
news. They were from the same town, south of Fort Sill, and
according to Net, Jakewad was famous there.

"I know you, man," Net told Jakewad, after hearing his
real name in the Reception Battalion. "You're the guy that
gave it to that cheerleader."

Jakewad glared at him.

"I'm from Lawton. I went to Macarthur like two years
after you," Net said.

"Okay," Jakewad said, sticking out his hand. "Cool, man.
But listen, she wasn't a cheerleader. She was just some girl,
okay?"

"Sure," Net said. He shook Jakewad's hand hard. He opened his mouth like he was going to say something else, but DS Burn, or DS Pissed as we liked to call him, was already moving us inside for haircuts.

Later that night, all of us in Black Hawks sorted ourselves into our bunks and swapped stories about why we'd joined the Army. My bunkmate was Cory, a big guy who wanted to be a soldier bad.

"Reserves is fucking bullshit," he told me when I said I wasn't a full enlistee. "You're either a soldier or a pussy. You can't be both." He shook his head with the same weighty disappointment that my mother had in the weeks before I left for BCT. "I'm sharing my bunk with Specialist Pussy," Cory told the room.

That's how I got my platoon nickname.

Net was also in the reserves, but he was smart enough not to advertise it. "After the army, I want to be a chef," he said.

A couple of the guys snickered.

"Yeah, it's not so bad. "I work at this Chinese food place back home. The chef there was a white guy. I asked him where he learned to cook because I was tired of wiping down tables and he said he learned in the Army. I figure if I get enough KP, I can get a chef job when I'm out. I'm up all fucking night anyway. I might take chaplain training, too. You get ten grand, just for taking the lousy chaplain course."

"Yeah, but you don't get to have sex anymore, man," Jakewad said.

Everyone got quiet.

I looked down the barracks aisle. Everyone was staring at the floor. It was weird enough that we were all in the same blue and white army sweats, sporting the same haircut. The silence was too much.

"Why are you a 13b?" I asked Jakewad. "Wanted to stay in Oklahoma?"

Net laughed. Lawton was a piece of shit town. Not much better than Faxton, where I was from.

"No," Jakewad said, real calm. He was always real calm. I knew he'd make a good soldier. "I'm too tall to fly helicopters. That's what I wanted to do. I'm a couple inches over the height limit. So I told my recruiter I'd go wherever they needed me. I've got good vision. Pilot vision. I'll be a good shooter."

"Bullshit, I bet you're running from the cops, aren't you, man?" a guy from another squad asked.

Thirty pairs of eyes focused on Jakewad. He shook his head.

"You really do that girl, or what?" the guy pressed.

Jakewad looked at the ceiling, and then back at the guy who was asking all the questions.

Net jumped in before Jakewad could answer. "Tell us how you got out of doing any jail time. C'mon." Net leaned into Jakewad. "It's a great fucking story. This guy's a legend back home."

Soon everyone was sitting up straight prodding Jakewad to tell the story. He flapped his arms to quiet us down. "Fine, fine," he said. "Shut the hell up already."

He paused like it was going to be a long one, so I moved to the floor and propped my head against the metal leg of Voodoo's bunk.

"So okay. It happened, whatever. And then I left, you know. I was," Jakewad looked around the room for the right word, "intoxicated? I slept it off in the outfield at Macarthur. When I woke up, I was freaking the fuck out. I didn't know what she was going to do, so I just went home to get my car. It was summer break and I figured I'd get out of Dodge for a while. I got this uncle in Texas."

Jakewad paused and ran a hand over his freshly buzzed hair. We were all touching our hair a lot.

"When I got there, there were these dudes on my porch. At first, I thought it was the law, so I started to run away. But they tackled me and started kicking me. Turns out, it was her brother and her cousins. I guess she told them, and they wanted to kill me. Good thing I was still a little drunk, or it would have hurt like a bitch. But they kicked my ass, seriously. I had like three broken ribs, a broken nose, and bruises fucking everywhere."

"No wonder your ass is so ugly," said Voodoo.

"Did she call the cops?" I asked

"No. I took pictures with my webcam of me all fucked up and sent them to her. I said that if she called the cops on me, I'd call the cops on them. I never heard from her again. It's been like three years, so I figure I'm safe."

"Fucking statute of limitations, man!" someone yelled.

The whole time Jakewad talked, I thought about Carolyn, my first girlfriend—my only girlfriend. She was fourteen when I was seventeen. Just a kid, really, but mature. And smart too. She didn't have any kid's body either. I was ready to see how it worked, but she just kept saying no, she wasn't ready. I think she was just scared of getting pregnant like her older sister did when she was sixteen.

We would be lying together, almost naked, and I could feel the heat of her through her panties. I always had condoms, just in case. But we'd end up just rubbing against each other and I'd be so close—so goddamn close. I knew it would feel so good, that it would make her feel good too if I just did it, just let her see how the two of us would feel together. But I never did anything.

When she didn't let me have it after junior prom, I left her and that slutty black dress in the hotel room I'd paid sixty bucks for. I went into town, already drunk, and sat at the bar until this blond woman started chatting me up.

"You a secret agent or something?" she asked. I was still in my tux.

"Yeah," I said, "Sure, I'm a secret agent." I bought her a couple of shots of whiskey, and she let me do it to her in the back room of the bar—no condom or anything. She was old and her hair felt like straw, but I was past ready.

When we were done I went back to the hotel and cuddled up next to Carolyn. She broke up with me soon after that. I left for BCT when I turned eighteen.

"What's the problem, Pussy? You never seen a girl naked?" Cory said.

"Pussy?" Voodoo asked.

"I guess Pussy never got no pussy," Net said.

••••

The next day we started phase one, the "red" phase of training, which lasted three weeks. During red phase we ran uphill, downhill, with our guns and gear, in the heat, and in the rain. When we weren't running, we were cleaning the barracks, or getting dropped for push-ups by DS Pissed. He dropped us as a platoon, in squads, in pairs. He dropped us because someone left their locker unlocked, because someone didn't shine their shoes the right way, because someone looked him in the eye, but mostly, he dropped us just to drop us.

An important part of red phase was working with our battle buddy, the other half of our two-man teams. I got teamed up with Jakewad because it turned out our birthdays were one day apart. We did our drills together and swapped items from our MREs. Mostly, we worked and slept, but we did have some time to get to know each other between drills and classes on navigation, international customs, and hygiene. He was actually a pretty nice guy. And a good soldier, like I thought he'd be. No one bothered him about the girl again until the seminar on sexual harassment.

Basically, the seminar was a boring lecture and a bunch of cheesy videos, the point of which was that we should all be careful not to harass the female recruits and that no means no, and so on.

There were about a hundred of us in the seminar room, all sitting with our platoons. At the end, the instructor, who was a woman, asked us all to share what we thought would be clear signals that someone was interested in engaging in sexual activity with us. Somebody from a platoon called the Morticians stood up and said, "If you make your expectations clear and she gives her consent." He was just kissing ass. Those words were right from the seminar and no one talks like that in real life.

"That's right, Specialist," the instructor said, "but what about some things that are maybe...less official. Perhaps something that's happened in your personal experience?"

Everyone started poking Jakewad and whispering that he should listen closely so he wouldn't get in trouble again.

"Battle Hawk platoon? Do you all have something to share?" the instructor said.

Everyone looked at Jakewad, who looked like he wanted to just stay quiet. I stood up instead.

"Yes, Specialist. Tell us about a time you received a clear 'yes' message in an intimate moment," said the instructor

I thought about how Carolyn's bucking hips seemed to say yes as much as Lydia, the lady from the bar, had when she'd said, "That's right. Show me you're a big man." But I didn't think I should tell either of those stories.

"With my high school girlfriend, I knew she was ready because she said, 'I want you' and 'Let's make love,'" I said. I knew it sounded cheesy and the guys would probably be all over me for it, but I didn't know what else to say. Carolyn never said yes, and I didn't think anyone else would understand what happened that night with Lydia.

When I sat back down, Jakewad turned around and nodded at me as if to say "thank you." I nodded back. The truth was that it wasn't as easy as they were making it seem in the

72

seminar. Sometimes girls said no just to say no when they really wanted to say yes. Sometimes people don't even know what they want until they get it.

•••

For four hours that night Jakewad and I had fire guard together. Now that wood stoves were extinct, fire guard seemed a little stupid, but we kept an eye out for thieves or soldiers walking alone, and ate honey-lemon flavored cough drops like they were candy.

"You still got that girlfriend?" Jakewad asked. "The one you *made love* to?"

"No," I said. It felt okay to tell him the truth. We were alone and it was 0300. It was the right time to reveal secrets. "I made that shit up. I lost it to a drunk thirty year old at a bar."

"Yeah?"

"Yeah. Carolyn was the girlfriend. She never gave it up. We broke up, anyway," I said.

Jakewad nodded. "That sucks, man. You love her?"

"I don't know," I said. I didn't know. "What about you? And that girl Net's always talking about. Were you dating her?"

"Kind of. Not really. We were just hanging out."

It seemed like he didn't want to tell me, but I thought if I stayed quiet he might start talking.

"We drank a case of beer. My brother had just passed me down his fake ID and it worked. I just wanted to celebrate," he said.

I had felt the same way at prom. Carolyn was wearing these stockings that ended in tight black bands on her thighs. I was in a tie.

"She was cool with the making out, and some other stuff. But I couldn't stop. I was so fucking horny. I just knew I had to do it, or I would die," Jakewad continued. He was picking at a scab on his wrist. He got it when Net swung his rifle at

73

him on one of our runs. DS Pissed dropped us all for twenty. We could have killed Net for that; we were already so sore. But Jakewad stayed calm, even though he had to do his push-ups on an injured wrist. It was hard to picture him being out of control at all, let alone raping anybody. Though nobody ever said "rape." It seemed to me that she had to have given him some clue that it was okay, the kind of clue I'd been waiting for on all those hot nights with Carolyn.

"Did she fight you?" I asked. "Or did she just say no in a confident voice with confident body posture?" This was a quote from our sexual harassment seminar. It was supposed to make him laugh.

"No, man. It wasn't like that. She just kept saying please in this quiet voice. Over and over again." Jakewad was looking off, but not for thieves or fires. He was watching himself do it to her. I could tell.

"Did you think after a while she was saying please, like please give it to me?" I asked. This is what I always knew would happen with Carolyn, if only I'd had the balls to try.

"No, man," Jakewad said. He shook his head. "It wasn't like that at all. Not at all."

The way he said it made my stomach drop. I unwrapped a cough drop and sucked on it loudly so I wouldn't have to say anything. I didn't know what to say.

• • • •

When we finally got to fire our weapons, during the "white" phase of training, we had already been eating and sleeping with them for five weeks. The range was muddy, but the sky was clear. "Good visibilty," Jakewad said. He squinted into the distance. He was always making a big deal about his vision. The targets at the end of the range were big black and white bulls-eyes. Somebody had put a turban on each one. That was to make us angry, DS Pissed said.

But the only person I was angry at was Jakewad. I had this

really clear idea of how things would have gone with Carolyn if I'd manned up, and now he'd fucking ruined it. Now, when it got to be late at night and the soldiers in the other bunks were breathing heavy, all I could think of were the scared eyes Carolyn made when we watched slasher movies. I hadn't masturbated in weeks.

I was in charge of handling Jakewad's ammo while he fired. He spent like twenty shells jerking around trying to knock the turbans off the targets. He only got one. Most guys didn't take the shooting too seriously. The range was already backed up, so we all knew we'd be kicked off as soon as we got a qualifying score, and this was the only part of our training that didn't make us sweat or sore. Net and Voodoo, who got paired up as battle-buddies, were taking turns trying to hit a tree stump ten yards behind the targets. They wanted to show off their accuracy without getting a passing score. We weren't supposed to think of our weapons as toys, but after spending so much time hauling them around unloaded, in complete safety, it was hard to take them seriously.

When I got sick of Jakewad playing around, I told him to use his goddamn pilot eyes to hit the target already, if he even could. He fired six straight rounds into the center of the bulls-eye.

"Sorry, Pussy," he said, and clicked the safety on his weapon. He gestured for me to take his place as shooter.

I didn't get hard shooting like Jakewad and the other guys. I was just hoping to get some down time, and eventually hit my marks. It took me a few rounds to get the hang of the M-16. It was light, but it still kicked back on me a bit. Even if I knew the first shot was too high, it would jerk my shoulder back and I couldn't correct as easily as I thought I'd be able to.

Jakewad was pissing me off on purpose, tossing a new magazine at my feet before I'd even emptied the old one, like he knew I'd miss. "Back off, asshole," I said.

I tried picturing Jakewad as the bulls-eye. I thought it

might motivate me to shoot straighter. It just made me angry.

"I don't know what your problem is, man. I'm just giving you the ammo so you can take your next thousand shots," he said.

"Fuck you, Jakewad," I said. Apparently, I said it loud enough for DS Pissed to hear. One time they definitely don't want you fighting with your battle buddy is when you have a loaded M-16.

"If you two fucks want to fight, you do it on your own time. Battle Hawks! Weapons down! Drop and give me thirty!"

We did.

We all got up, rubbing our triceps. DS Pissed and the range supervisors were in the jeeps. Our time on the range was up. We loaded our weapons, but DS Pissed wouldn't let us climb in.

"Thanks to your battling buddies there you'll all be walking back to barracks tonight," he said. "Chow closes at oh-seven-hundred."

Then the jeeps were sounds in the distance, and we knew we really were walking our sore asses back to barracks.

"Fuck, man," Net said to me. "What the fuck?"

I shrugged. I didn't feel like apologizing. I figured this was Jakewad's fault.

"Seriously, Pussy, you got to keep that shit contained," Cory said.

"Whatever," I said. "Maybe if I didn't have a fucking *rapist* as a battle buddy." Like I said, rape was one word we did not say. Doing it to, giving it to, and fucking were things you did to your girlfriend. "Rape" was something you secretly worried might happen to her. "He told me he raped her," I said, looking at Jakewad. "She said 'please' and he wouldn't stop. Probably held her down and everything." I spat in the grass.

Jakewad's calm soldier exterior didn't so much melt as light up like flash paper and disappear. He came at me hard, but I was ready. I didn't give two shits about him or his stupid vision, or even my goddamn battle-buddy responsibilities. At night, when I wanted to think about doing it to Carolyn, all I could think about was him doing it to her and her asking him to stop. It was too much to take.

Jakewad threw a punch that landed on my shoulder. It hurt like a bitch, but I swung and got him on the jaw with a left hook. The guys in our platoon were around us like ants on a popsicle stick, but they weren't stopping us. I think they knew we just needed to get it out.

When we were finally on the ground, Jakewad had me pinned and was hitting me on the back of my head with his fists. I didn't care if he killed me. He'd already taken everything he could from me. "Look, man, I'm sorry," he kept saying, as he pounded my skull with his fists. "I'm fucking sorry." I didn't know who he was apologizing to or when, if ever, I would find out.

The News and What it Means to Noah

1995: While Noah is finishing his B.S. in particle physics at MIT, two scientists in Colorado produce the first quantity of Bose-Einstein Condensate. His advisor has been working on the same experiment, laser-cooling atoms of sodium-23 until the vapor stabilizes for a moment, then evaporates into nothing. Noah asks him if he's going to continue his experiment, now that the desired result has already been achieved. "Of course," his advisor says in his thick German accent. "Your father made love to your mother, yes? Does this mean you should never make love to a beautiful woman?"

2000: In Fermilab, outside Chicago, the DONUT collaboration finds definitive evidence of Tau neutrino interactions. Now the only particle present in the proposed standard model but missing in experiments is the Higgs Boson, the God Particle. The news is all over Cornell, where Noah is starting his PhD. He left his girlfriend, Jenny, behind in Massachusetts, spitting platitudes about distance and timing and what was right for his career. He wonders if she is aware of this news, of how his whole world is different now. He copies the formula into his notebook:

$$\sigma^{const}(\nu_\tau) = 2.51 n^{1.52} \times 10^{-40} \text{cm}^2 \text{ GeV}^{-1} \text{ for } n \geq 4$$
where n is the controlling parameter for the differential.

Jenny was not a scientist, but for some reason Noah imagines her studying the equation along with him, trying to determine how these mesons, these charmed particles, and a few nanoseconds of decay could combine into something so amazing.

2002: Celia, a fifth year PhD student, tells him about the antihydrogen being produced at CERN. "It's low-energy," she says. "How low energy?" he asks. "I think they're getting like a twentieth of a second before it hits the wall." They are smoking pot on the lawn behind the student center. Celia has covered her shoes with little drawings of atomic symbols. As they talk about the antihydrogen, she scribbles h-bars on her dingy shoelaces. Noah thinks he is probably in love with her. "You know what we should do?" she says, smoke pouring out of her open mouth like a cauldron. "We should open a pub, and call it 'H-Bar.' Get it?" Noah smiles and inhales. When he licks his lips he can taste the cigarette paper and the faintest hint of her lip gloss. A twentieth of a second isn't very long, but Noah understands that it is long enough.

2004: The Nobel Prize in Physics goes to a trio of Americans for their discovery of asymptotic freedom during high energy particle interactions. Noah's own research on leptons has hit a wall. Under other circumstances, Noah might be wandering the halls of the physics department in a fog of depression, but Celia has finally come around on letting him call her his girlfriend. That was her phrase, "come around." It reminds Noah of when he first learned the difference between fermions and bosons. He asked his professor the same questions over and over again, *How can something turn only half way around and be exactly where it started? How can something need to turn around twice before you are looking at its face again?* He still doesn't have satisfying answers to these questions, but he's accepted the fact that, even in science where everything is supposed to be measurable and certain, some questions do not have answers.

2007: A pair of German physicists claim to have broken the light barrier by jumping a couple of microwave photons across three meters of space instantly. The headline that comes through the listserv to Noah's email address at Princeton says, "Is Time Travel Possible?" This kind of discovery should have him jumping out of his skin with excitement, but it barely registers. He reads the article on his laptop in bed. Celia is curled around his numb left arm. She's given up a research fellowship in Sweden to stay with him. Even if he could travel to any moment—past, present or future—how could he possibly choose to be anywhere but right here?

2008: This year the Nobel Prize goes to three Japanese scientists for their groundbreaking work in spontaneous symmetry breaking. The system requires outcomes of relatively equal probability, like the two possible outcomes of an early-indicator, easy-to-read, digital home pregnancy test. If the system is sampled, one of the two outcomes must occur. In Noah's case: positive, negative. Since the probability of one outcome rises to 1, while the probability of the other falls to 0, the system is no longer symmetric. The indicators of the former symmetry are still present, however. For his part, Noah can almost see himself and Celia sighing with relief, hugging each other hard, making love right there on the bathroom mat, laughing as he rolls on the condom. However, the evidence records a different outcome: the locked bathroom door, the dry salt on her cheeks, the clinic bill divided evenly between them—down to the last penny.

2008: The Large Hadron Collider opens at CERN and the list to get in and mine data is a thousand miles long. When they turn the machine on for the first time, it's like turning on a light in a dark room. Suddenly, there is endless potential for discovery, surprise, confirmation. It happens just as Noah's relationship with Celia finally falls apart. Reams of new formulas are being published every day. When he can no longer stand being stuck in slow motion as the rest of the world seems to be picking up speed, Noah writes a few equations of his own.

$$\{i\delta\partial/\partial\Psi\ (r,\ t) = C\Psi = (-\delta/2m\ \nabla^2 + N(r)\ )$$
$$\{\Psi\ (r,\ t) = -\delta^2/2m\nabla^2\Psi\ (r,\ t) + N(r)\Psi(r,\ t)$$
$$\{C\Psi(r) = -\delta^2/2m(r) + N(r)\Psi(r)$$

where C is Celia, N is Noah, Ψ is the constant of common feelings, r is small romantic gestures, and δ is what he must solve for. δ is the thing he could not predict, the thing he still doesn't understand.

2009: The Higg's Boson has been eliminated in most of the possible weight spectrum. The article, which is subtitled "Are You There God Particle? It's Us, Science," cites 90–95% confidence in each interval. Noah can't remember the last time he was 90% confident in anything, so he finds these numbers very convincing. He makes a chart in one of his graph paper notebooks. It's a confidence curve plotted to 95%. He fills it in as follows:

Celia was the right woman for me: (1, 50): 50%
Celia was the wrong woman for me: (2, 50): 50%
The baby was mine: (3, 66): 66%
There is no Higgs Boson in the measurable
   spectrum: (4, 95): 95%

Staring at the graph, its graceful rise and fall, makes him feel more certain, and more uncertain than he has ever been.

2011: This time it's Italian scientists who claim to have pushed particles past the speed of light. They've used neutrinos, the ghostly particles that can travel right through solid matter, so they could test the speed over a much longer distance. After six months of confirming the results, no one attached to CERN, OPERA or the LHC can find any error. *Is this it?* Noah wonders. The big news outlets are predicting the end of the standard model, the death of special relativity, the collapse of modern particle physics, but of course they're overreacting. Special relativity can permit superluminosity, it just makes things more complicated. Even some of his scientist friends react like the universe is unraveling before their eyes. *But look around*, he implores them, *everything is just the same as it was before*. Nothing has changed.

He does think, though, once again about the possibility of time travel. If the results are accurate, it could mean quantum tunneling. It could mean extra dimensions. It could mean a new brane universe model. In any of these instances, it would be possible to leave a place, race around a bit, and return before you left. And this time, Noah knows exactly where he would go.

No System for Blindness

••••••••••••••••••••••••••

Three weeks after my father loses his vision, I get the first phone call. The day manager at the coffee house, Jeanne, knows about the situation with my father. She lets me slip out the back for unauthorized breaks when my cell phone rings.

"Hello," the voice on the line says. "Is this Marie Carroll?"

"Yes," I say. "Is this about my father?"

"No. I'm calling from Publishers' Sweepstakes," he says. "Your credit card company entered you in a drawing to thank you for your good credit history. Your name was chosen as one of our ten finalists." He pauses for a reaction.

"Really?" I ask. I want to sound skeptical, but the reverb of my voice in the earpiece sounds coy, almost flirtatious.

"Really!" he says. "A drawing will be held on May seventh to determine the winner. Each of the ten finalists will receive five thousand dollars, and the grand prize winner will win a million dollars!"

"Okay." I wait for him to ask me for something—a portion of the taxes up front, a certified check, my credit card number. But he doesn't, and I don't hang up.

"You don't sound excited," he says.

"Is this, like, a scam?" I ask. It's a silly question, I realize even as I'm asking it.

"No," he says. "This is Publishers'. You've heard of Publishers', right?"

It sounds partially right, vaguely familiar. I say, "Yes." I think I have.

"Great. Let me tell you about all the things you've already won."

He slips easily into a lengthy description of what he calls "my vacation package." "No time-share presentations," he says. "A choice of any of twenty-six vacation spots in the U.S. and abroad." "A free year of magazine subscriptions." It doesn't feel real, but listening to it is better than working: releasing coffee from spring-loaded pour spouts, identifying scones for puzzled customers, the constant pointing to the creamer station.

When the voice stops I say, "Okay."

"I just have to verify some of your information."

This is it, I think. He will ask for my social security number, my mother's maiden name. I see blank bank statements, overdue credit-card notices, a car note for a vehicle I've never seen.

"Are you still at 4116 Stilmore Road?" he asks.

"Yes."

He recites my telephone number and e-mail address. Finally, he rattles off my credit card number, complete with expiration date. "Is that right?"

"Yes," I say.

"Great. I'll give you an eight-hundred number to call in case you have any questions. My supervisor will call back within the next few hours to firm everything up."

I punch the eight-hundred number into my cell phone.

"One more thing, Marie. When my supervisor calls, he's going to ask you to rate me on a scale of one to five. It's for promotions and stuff. Will you put in a good word for me? My name's Chad."

When I go back inside, there is no line and Jeanne is changing the coins in the tip jar for dollar bills from the register.

"Everything okay?" she asks.

"Fine," I say. "Maybe better."

There looks to be about seventeen dollars in the tip jar. It is a good amount for one shift, and I still have about an hour left, but I have bigger numbers in my head.

I tell her about the magazine subscriptions, the free vacation, the follow-up phone call I am expecting. The million dollars.

"Sounds like a scam," she says.

"I know. That's what I thought at first. But the guy already has my credit-card number. He knew a lot of my information."

"So?"

"So, it seems official. If he's trying to rip me off, why doesn't he just buy stuff with my credit card? I'm not sure what he could want that he doesn't already have."

I don't know if I believe what I'm saying. But now that I've said it out loud, it sounds convincing.

"So you think you're going to win a million dollars, huh?"

"No," I say. "But the free vacation would be cool anyway."

"Oh yeah?" Jeanne changes a palmful of dimes for a dollar bill. "You don't even go out for drinks after work. You gonna take your dad on the trip with you?" she asks, laughing.

••••

Three weeks before, I was surprised to find my father still in bed at eight in the morning. I knocked on the door.

"Dad?" I said.

He looked toward me but not at me, and then reached for his glasses. He grasped them on the second try and slid them on. "Marie?" he asked. "Is it daytime?"

As always, we remained calm. Since my father was diagnosed with Multiple Sclerosis nine years ago, I had mastered the art of remaining calm. He didn't want to go to the emergency room, so I called his doctor.

I reported back: "It's called optic neuritis. She said the double vision and blind spots you were having were probably leading up to this. We should have gone in a few days ago."

He nodded, facing me. His eyes blinked wildly. He still had his glasses on—useless, but familiar. I was glad he was wearing them. When I came into his room that morning his face looked naked without them. "What do we do now?"

I pushed a handful of pills into his damp palm—tiny white Dilantin diamonds, green and white Antivert tablets, Neurontins—orange like my father's old hunting vest and smooth as the gelatin caplets that burst into sponges in water. "Take these. She wants to give you a steroid treatment as soon as possible. It'll bring down the swelling behind your eyes and release the pressure on the nerve."

He stopped blinking.

"It'll help," I said.

"Okay. When should we go?"

"Soon. Now. The sooner the better."

"I have to go to the bathroom."

Our house, it seemed, was prepared for everything but this. When a patient has Multiple Sclerosis, they can't treat the real disease—his immune system attacking his brain. They can only treat the symptoms. We were ready for my father's typical attacks. But not this.

"How long does it usually last?" I'd asked his doctor.

"Maybe a few hours, maybe months."

"Months?"

"You know how it is Marie," she said, "There's just no way to know."

What she didn't say, but I already knew was that any of his attack symptoms could become permanent at any time.

••••

I spend the day catching up on three weeks of errands. On the way home, I call the doctor. It's been long enough that I need to know what our options are.

"If this turns out not to be a temporary thing, is there anything we can do?"

"Of course," she says. My heart lifts. "We have physical therapists who can help your father learn to do things a new way. There are counselors available for your father, and you, to help you deal with the changes."

"No." She doesn't understand. "I mean, medically. Is there a surgery for this or anything?"

"Not at this time. It's not something we can treat beyond trying to take down the swelling."

"What about a medical trial? Maybe there's something that hasn't been approved yet."

"I'm sorry, Marie. There isn't."

"We have really good insurance."

"It's not a financial issue," she says. "There isn't anything we can do right now. Try to stay positive. Remember, we don't worry about possibilities. We deal with realities."

When I get home, Dad is on the couch, but the television is off.

"Can you see anything?" I ask.

He shakes his head. "Not right now. But I saw a few minutes of the game this afternoon. Would you believe it, right when my eye came in they cut to commercial."

"Figures," I say.

"There anything new out there I should know about? A new color or something?"

"No," I say. "Same old."

"Would you do me a favor?" he asks.

There is a vulnerability in his voice that tells me this isn't an ordinary favor (change a light bulb, bring in his pills or show him, again, how to turn on the computer). Maybe be wants me to bring in my baby pictures so he could look at them if his vision comes back. Maybe he'll ask me to read him something from Edgar Allen Poe. Or maybe when I bring in dinner, he'll want me to describe it to him first.

He says, "Would you cut my nails for me? They're really getting in my way."

I should have known better. This is the man whose last anniversary date was for dinner and an oil change.

"Sure," I say.

While I'm trimming his nails, my cell phone rings, flashing the same area code as before. I excuse myself, leaving my dad stretched out on the sofa, right hand dangling over a blue plastic grocery bag. I step out onto the porch. It is cool, but not cold. I can just see my breath bouncing off the mouthpiece.

"Hello?"

"Hi. Marie Carroll? This is Bob with Publishers'."

"Hi."

"I know you spoke with Chad this afternoon. How would you rate him in terms of being friendly and informative? On a scale of one to five."

"Five," I say.

"Great. Let me just review what we'll be sending you by certified mail in the next two weeks."

He rattles off the list—the vacation package, the information about the million dollar drawing, the year of magazine subscriptions.

"We've assembled a sampling of magazines for you based on your profile. Would you like to hear a complete list?"

"No thanks," I say. "Whatever you've got down is fine."

"Okay then," he says. "We do ask that you help us out with the shipping costs of your magazine subscriptions. That will come out to two-ten a month. If you like I can go ahead and charge your Visa card for that right now. Do I have your permission to do that?"

"Um. No," I say.

"Pardon me?"

"Can you just not send them?"

"I assure you this is much less than the actual cost of the magazines themselves, plus everything else you're getting. Would you like to pay another way?"

"No."

"I can't send anything unless I have your permission to bill you for the shipping and handling costs."

"No," I say. "I don't want to pay for anything until I see something in writing about all this."

"Have a nice day," he says. His final words get quieter as he speaks, as if he is already moving the receiver down to its cradle. Then, click, flat silence. I blow into the phone, sending a static sound back into my own ear. I stand this way for a while, waiting for my mind to catch up to the end of the conversation.

When it does, I feel disappointed, even though I knew it probably wasn't real. It is the same feeling I had four months ago when I last made plans to see my mother. Dad was having a routine overnight at the MS clinic. Mom said she'd be by in the morning for coffee then called when the coffee was already cold and growing thick in the pot, the cream warm in its ceramic pitcher, to say she'd slept late and would be by for dinner instead. She called again at seven. By then I'd already eaten half of the spaghetti I'd made, one cold, thin noodle at a time, standing up at the stove, scraping my tongue on the crusty clots of sauce. She said she was sorry, she was just packing up to leave work. She'd be here in an hour. I had just finished cleaning the coffee pot and scooping brown crystals into the new filter when she called to say she didn't realize it was so late. She was going to head home to bed. She'd be by, she promised, some time soon. I listened to the silence on the other end of the line for a few minutes after she hung up. I thought it sounded like her.

I make a lot of noise on my way back into the living room so I don't surprise my dad. He is running his fingernails along the pad of his thumb, feeling the differences between long and short and the tingling of freshly exposed skin.

"Who was on the phone?" he asks.

"No one," I say. "Give me your hand."

"Long conversation for no one." He thrusts his hand toward me, missing my outstretched palm by six inches. "A boy?"

"No," I say. "No one." I snap the nail off his little finger with the dull nail clippers. I feel foolish for believing it at all. I'm glad I haven't told Dad.

"You know it's okay for you to tell me when your mother calls."

"I know, Dad. It wasn't Mom."

He sits up, turns his head toward me. "It was back for a second," he says. "But now it's gone." He rubs his left eye with his left hand. "Darn. I really wanted to see you." He pauses just long enough for me to think he misses my face. "I can never tell when you're lying," he says.

He tucks his right hand against his body and rolls over onto his arm. He offers me his left hand. I insert his thumbnail into the clippers. I try to keep my own hand steady, though I am already crying.

Dad says, "Will you put the news on?"

I do. I am happy to. I haven't cried in front of my dad since I was fourteen and split my chin open slipping on some ice. I steadily trim his remaining nails. I keep my staccato breathing quieter than the television. When I need extra cover, I rustle the trash bag. The crying only lasts about five minutes, but I look my father right in the eyes the whole time.

· · · ·

I am amazed at how quickly the crying becomes a habit for me. I sit next to him on the couch while he listens to baseball. I cry quietly, pretending to talk to him about all the things we never talk about. His eyes, though useless, never look glassy or lifeless. There is always emotion behind them. I match the fake conversation to his emotions.

When our pitcher has a bad game his eyes are soft, his cheeks slack. I imagine I am telling him, "I have these memories of you coaching my softball team. You could throw the ball in the air and hit it to any girl on the field. But I hated softball. I dreaded those moments when you'd hit the ball to me and it would fall behind me in the dirt. I didn't want to be there. I don't know what to do with these memories now."

It starts to feel like he understands, and the crying comes more and more naturally to me. It feels overdue. Good.

May seventh comes and goes with no phone call from Chad or Bob. No news about the Publishers' drawing. But I still have the eight-hundred number in my phone. I help my dad get dressed and into the kitchen, then go out to the porch before breakfast. I call the number. It rings and rings, but I am not giving up.

When someone finally picks up I say, "Is this Publishers'?"

"Yes it is. This is Brad. How can I help you?"

"My name's Marie Carroll. I was told I was a finalist for the May seventh drawing and I hadn't heard anything—"

"Okay ma'am. Can I have your finalist number?"

"I don't have one. No one gave me one."

"You should have gotten it in the mail. Did you send in your official entry form?"

"No. I was told I was already entered. I talked to Chad and Bob. Are they there?"

"You never sent in your entry form?"

"No. I never got it," I say.

"The form should have come in the initial mailer with the information about your free vacation and your first month of magazines. Did you pay the shipping and handling fee?"

"No," I say.

"No? Well, you're in luck ma'am. There's another million dollar drawing in three weeks and if you'll put in a good word for me, I can put you in the computer for it. How does that sound?"

"Does it cost money?"

"Absolutely not. Just the shipping fee for your magazines. That'll get that entry form to you."

"Chad said that as a finalist I'd already won five thousand dollars. Is that true?"

"You only get that money if you're not chosen as our million dollar winner. So we really need that entry form. Marie Carroll on Stilmore Road?"

"Yes."

"I have your information right here. Should I go ahead and charge your credit card for the shipping?"

"No," I say. He doesn't reply and I'm afraid he is going to hang up again. "I don't believe you."

"If you don't mind me saying so, maybe you should."

"What?"

"I'm looking at your credit history," he says. "School loans, late car payments. I'm seeing a lot of medical expenses."

"This is none of your business."

"Maybe not, but you know what I don't see? Dinners out. Movies. Plane tickets. This is a million dollars we're talking about. You're going to let that chance go because you don't want to pay three dollars for shipping?"

As Brad breathes on the other end of the line, I realize that my credit card company probably did sell them my information. I had been targeted because my situation looked desperate. I needed the money. I needed a change. I'm sure they thought I was the kind of person who'd believe anything, who needed to believe something.

Brad says, "This is the kind of money that will change your life."

But it is becoming clear to me that it won't. What I would need to change my life, you can't get with money.

••••

In the kitchen, my father pulls a donut from a box on the counter and makes his way back to the table. He uses an orthopedic cane to navigate the kitchen, though he knows the major obstacles well by now. I sit down across from him, look at him, and pretend to tell him about the phone call.

When the tears come, they don't surprise me. What surprises me is my father saying, "Are you crying?"

"No," I say. "Did you hear something?"

"I can see you," he says. "You look awful. What happened?"

I put my hands up, wiping my face and covering my mouth. But it is too late. I can't pretend anymore that I might soon be a millionaire. I can't pretend my crying has brought us closer together when I've been hiding it from him all this time.

"I got this phone call," I say. It is the first thing I can think of that doesn't involve him. "These guys said my credit card company entered me in a drawing and I could win a million dollars."

"You didn't give them your credit card number, did you?"

"No, Dad. I'm not stupid. I was just hoping it was real

I guess." It comes more easily than I expect. Perhaps all the practice I've had being honest in my head has helped.

"Oh," he says. "I'm sorry." He takes his glasses off and rubs his eyes. "It's gone again."

It occurs to me that I haven't seen my father cry since my mother left six years ago.

"It's okay," I say. "I wouldn't know what to do with the money anyway." It is the first true, sad thing I've said out loud to my father in a long time. We spend so much energy being strong for each other that we can't talk anymore about the things that make us weak.

He stares past me, to my left, tapping the table in search of his glasses. There is powdered sugar in his beard. It makes him look older. He places his glasses back on the bridge of his nose. There is a greasy white streak across one lens, but he can't see it.

I feel like crying again, but I stop myself. My dad wouldn't like it. And I am still hoping that his vision might come back, suddenly, and for good. And when it does, I want to be smiling.

Paradise Hardware

· ·

Dinner at Clarke Brite's house is spicy crab cakes with minted pineapple salsa, mashed potatoes, pink grapefruit, raw broccoli crowns and sparkling grape juice. Clarke hasn't tasted real champagne since Lisa checked *Taking Charge of Your Fertility (Revised Edition)* out of the library and found out alcohol is a male reproductive tract toxin. She says real champagne could make her fallopian tubes a hostile environment. Clarke replies: "Working at a bar probably isn't helping your fallopian tubes."

Clarke takes a bite of his crab cake.

Lisa says, "I added chick-peas to the recipe, for folic acid. It'll increase your sperm count."

He interrupts, "What's this brown stuff?"

"I also added some chocolate."

Clarke pushes his plate away and raises his napkin to his lips.

"Just a little bit," she says. "It is the best source of L-arginine. It makes your sperm more mobile. And," she emphasizes the "and," like Clarke needs to be sold, "Men with low levels of L-arginine have abnormal sperm. I learned that from a girl at work. She wasn't getting pregnant either and she started making her husband eat more chocolate. Nine months later, twins."

Lisa works the sunup shift at Fast Freddie's Bar and Grille. Her lungs are already coated with smoke from cheap flavored cigars and dust from the fog machine. But she says she's going to quit as soon as the pregnancy test is positive. "As soon as the line's there," she says, "I'm gone. The baby shouldn't be affected that early, but still. Just to be safe."

Now that Clarke has inherited the hardware store, Lisa's talking early retirement.

"Just sell it," she says.

"I can't." For a moment Clarke considers telling her how he feels about Elysian Hardware. How it makes him feel part of a simpler time. How, when he's there, he can forget about his mortgage, the paperwork he needs to file with Teleflora and all of the science behind making a baby. He can just be.

But instead he mutters, "I owe it to Uncle Leo to keep it."

Between bites of pink grapefruit containing lycopene, noted for raising men's sperm count, he tells Lisa how Leo never liquidated his stock. He never even emptied the cash register. He just locked the doors one day and never went back.

The story goes that Leo heard on the radio that North Carolina was going be the next Atlantis. Two hurricanes had already hit the Carolinas in two months when Leo started hearing warnings for hurricane Ione. He was certain that was going to be the end and moved his whole family up to Pennsylvania in a hurry. When Clarke got the news of his inheritance, the doors of Elysian Hardware hadn't been opened since they'd been closed in 1955.

"If you sold it," Lisa says, "maybe you could hire another arranger for the flower store and you wouldn't even have to work there. You could just manage it."

Clarke says: "It's my store. I'm not selling it."

Lisa rolls her eyes and puts a plate of nuts on the table. They are almonds and peanuts for vitamin E. They should protect Clarke's sperm membranes from free radical damage, and enhance fertilization ability. "What about the stuff in it?"

Clarke nods and Lisa smiles. She reminds Clarke of a single long-stemmed rose in a bud vase with her smooth red hair and thin hips.

She takes a shot of cough syrup.

"Doesn't that stuff have alcohol in it? I thought that was a no-no."

"Robitussin will loosen the mucus on my cervix to let sperm through."

"Is that really true?" He asks.

Lisa nods. "Just like lungs."

For some reason, Clarke can no longer think about sex. Instead he thinks about the first time he brought Lisa to the hardware store. Clarke loved the name "Elysian" because it meant paradise. It wasn't until later that he found out Thompson Street used to be Elysian Road and the store was simply named for its address. But for him, it was a paradise. A simple place, untouched by certain complications. He had taken Lisa with him to take her mind off the baby. He hoped that the store would be something they could take care of together. But she didn't seem as intrigued as Clarke was.

She walked around as if she were shopping, pointing to things she liked: quilted gardening gloves, packets of vegetable seeds, decorative door knobs. He had been eager to explain things to her. "This," he told her, "is an old raccoon trap. They don't sell them anymore because they aren't safe."

She laughed at him, saying, "What do you know about raccoon traps? You make bouquets."

He felt this was somehow related to her not being pregnant. He told her she could take some things for the house if she wanted. She just shrugged and he ended up taking home an entire box of things he thought she might like. He brought the quilted gloves and a stone garden frog, and some blank keys because he thought they were interesting and mysterious, like his wife.

••••

Two months, six days, and a gain of almost eight thousand dollars later, Lisa still isn't pregnant. Clarke has switched to boxers because Lisa hypothesized that his briefs were pulling his testicles too close to his body, raising his sperm temperature and killing off all the good ones. She cited this same possible problem when she stopped allowing him to take hot showers. Now, whenever he is getting ready for work he can expect at least two drop-ins from Lisa making sure his shower water is unpleasantly tepid. She has also stopped having sex with him altogether except for the week when she is ovulating, saying that short periods of abstinence will increase the potency of his sperm. He is up to six pink grapefruits a week and has to disappear to Elysian Hardware in order to eat anything that isn't packed with oysters, avocados, or undercooked meats. She stopped letting him have burgers medium-well when she discovered that cooking meat will kill the bacteria that produce B12. A B12 deficiency could result in pernicious anemia, a serious threat to both his and her fertility. But Clarke has his sex drive back thanks to one very difficult compromise. Now, on the rare occasions that they do make love, they do it inside the hardware store. At first Lisa had completely rejected the idea, but Clarke convinced her that a more powerful orgasm from him would launch his sperm even closer to her fallopian tubes. And she agreed.

The store itself is more than half empty and Clarke has called the appraiser back in to find out what he has left that's worth anything.

"Does the cash register still work?"

Clarke nods.

The appraiser points to a brass plaque with the letters 'NCR' on it. "See that? National Cash Register company. They stopped making mechanical registers in 1953. Three-thousand dollars without breaking a sweat."

Clarke holds up a long, flat piece of metal with a crank on one side. It has NCR on it, too. "What's this thing?"

"That's a check writer. You could get about half as much for it."

"But how does it work?"

The appraiser shrugs. He is not interested in history, in putting together one of uncle Leo's Thursdays. He sees the prices, not the past. It's the same thing when he tries to tell Lisa about it. The other day he found a box of iron birdfeeders whose red, blue and white paint had turned to gray-ish red, gray-ish blue, and gray. He tried to remind Lisa of the first Fourth of July they'd spent together. He'd come to her house early in the afternoon and surprised her with irises. They didn't make it to the fireworks. Instead they made love for hours on Lisa's enclosed back porch. With the flowers and the cool breezes and the sex, he thought, this just had to be love.

That was before he inherited the hardware store. Before any talk of a baby. Now they only see each other at dinner where he chokes down pink grapefruits and they set a time around the middle of the month to meet at Elysian and try and make a baby.

You think you've got it all: flowers, sunshine, a house on Robin Street and a portal back to 1955. That doesn't mean you're in love. It's a trick, like the cheap gold letters they use at the flower shop. You take the way people in movies look at sunsets, you take the mean things your father used to say to your mother, you take page thirty-one from the kama sutra. You put them together. It is this easy.

"These light fixtures," the appraiser says, "are at least sixty-years old. This lantern might be even older. Do you know how to make it work?"

Clarke shrugs. He doesn't know how to make anything work anymore.

••••

After getting quotes for a mechanical lawnmower, the bathroom faucet, and one of the first bottles of super-glue, Clarke walks out with the appraiser, but he doesn't go home. He can't stand another night of corn and carrot chowder, dried beans and going to bed with Lisa tasting like cough syrup. He cannot eat one more pink grapefruit.

He walks around the back room of the hardware store and is surprised when he finds himself aroused. His body, he supposes, knows that this is the only place he has sex. He thinks about Lisa, back when they first met. Before she was force-feeding him Savoy cabbage and Brussels sprouts. He touches himself.

It isn't until he starts to look around for something soft that he sees Lisa, tall and still like a single rose in a bud vase. But this is not in his mind.

"You were just going to waste that." She says. "You were going to spray all that perfectly good sperm onto the floor, weren't you. Is that what you've been doing here all this time? Is this why I'm not pregnant?"

She looks like she might cry and Clarke tries his best to look like that. Devastated, or at least remorseful. But he doesn't feel it.

"Do you even want a baby?"

She looks at him, expecting, but there is nothing to say.

••••

Clarke spends the next three nights in the hardware store on an army surplus cot from 1951. He watches his surroundings slowly disappear as the appraiser comes in and removes things to auction off. He thinks about the way flowers look when he leaves them on the counter for a long weekend without water.

When he goes back home, he doesn't expect Lisa to be there, but he's tired of watching the past disappear and longing for something familiar. But she is there, packing things. He moves through the house, soundlessly, making himself a sandwich, noticing the missing flatware, sheets, and the paintings she'd bought at flea markets.

"Clarke," she calls.

He doesn't move. He can sense where her voice is coming from, but does not follow it. She comes into the kitchen. She is carrying a photograph, one Clarke hasn't seen in a long time. It is from four years ago, when they went to visit Uncle Leo in Pittsburgh. Their chins are large in the frame and the visible part of Clarke's elbow is closest to the camera. You can tell Leo, the photographer, is sitting below them. Lisa is wearing a photograph smile, the kind you put on when someone holds up a camera. But Clarke, who is looking at Lisa, not the lens, looks genuinely happy.

"Look at it," she commands.

He does.

"You loved me then. Look at your face. See for yourself."

He wants to tell her something about that day. That she is right, that he loved her, that he is capable of loving her. But he can't put anything together. The woman in the picture barely reminds him of the woman he woke up next to this morning. When he thinks about Lisa now, he can only see the empty hardware store.

She asks Clarke, "Is this the last time I'm ever going to see you?"

The way she says it, he almost rushes to take her in his

arms. He almost wants to try again. Sell the store and have a baby. Smile with her. But his Uncle Leo set this example for him fifty-three years ago: Get out before it all goes under, and you with it.

He nods and watches her leave. He turns on the radio so he doesn't have to hear the car start.

• • • •

Clarke drives down route seventeen to Thompson Street. He goes inside Elysian Hardware because he wants that feeling back of being able to try again, of getting to turn back the clock a little ways. But there is no escape left here, no capacity for transportation. It is empty, except for a note from the appraiser saying that they got fifty-four dollars for the radio and not to run the water because they've taken the pipes to sell to people who might need old parts.

Clarke sits down in the emptiness. He misses Lisa like he wants a drink of water, but there are no pipes.

The Disappearance of Maliseet Lake
••••••••••••••••••••••••••••••••••••••

Peter bangs on our door at 3:30 a.m., waking us up. "The lake is gone," he says.

The three of us go outside together. It is too early for sunlight but the moon illuminates a giant crater. I have trouble recognizing it as the lake at first. I thought of the lake as a symmetrical bowl, the sides gently sloping down to a consistent depth. But the opening before me has a geography all its own: hills, valleys, smaller craters. The dirt at the bottom is still wet and puddles fill the lowest elevations.

There is matter, too. The bottom of the lake is littered with leaves and twigs, a few big branches and fewer trees. There are colorful soda cans, tackle boxes, some lonely shoes. The wooden boats are smashed to planks. The fiberglass boats are mostly overturned. One stands nearly upright against the side of the bowl. There are engine parts about. Some fish, not as many as you would think, lie still in the crater, or thrash in the small puddles.

"It's gone," I say.

"I know," Peter says.

My husband, Smith, says, "Where did it go? All that water."

We stare at the hole for most of the morning. By four, all of the other fishers are outside in their heavy flannel shirts; tackle boxes in hand, poles ready. The other members of our small community slowly stream out of their houses as they wake up and notice the crowd. By half past five, nearly the whole town is standing outside. We form a distended ring around the lake, four bodies deep. For a long time, no one speaks. Then a man steps into the crater and a woman yells, "Stop!"

Everyone turns to look. The woman's expression turns from horror to embarrassment. She nods to the man, who is probably her husband, and he skids down the steep side of the lake into the crater, running to one of the overturned boats.

Another man goes in to help him roll it over. Then another man, to check his own boat. Soon, everyone is in the lake.

I follow Smith to the western end where the splintered pieces of our little green bait boat are scattered. Smith gathers them up. I do not know what to say so I help, my bare feet sticking in the thick mud. The green paint makes them easy to find. Here is a sun-bleached board from the top of the keel. Here is an algae-slick fragment from the boat's underbelly. Here is the torn plastic seat where Smith sits to fish.

The sun comes up and birds invade the basin. For us, the crater means emptiness; for them, a fortune had been laid bare. They swoop in, picking algae from the mud, tree limbs, garbage. They gulp down tiny fish dug out of the puddles with their beaks. A group of three takes turns pulling flesh off of one of the larger fish, lying still in the dirt.

By six the birds make it impossible for us to continue clearing the lake. Jackson Stoat calls a meeting at the town community center. "At nine," he says, "sharp. To talk about the lake." People pitch in to carry the fiberglass boats to shore, and then go back home to wait.

•••

I fix breakfast for me and Smith and get dressed for work.

"Where are you going?" he asks when I emerge from the bedroom in pants and a collared shirt.

"Work," I say. "It's Thursday."

"You can't go today. There's a meeting."

"Since when do you care about town meetings?"

"Since I had to pick my goddamn boat up a splinter at a time from the empty goddamn lake. That's since when."

I dip my spoon into my oatmeal and pull it back out.

"No one's going to work today," he says.

He's probably right. Ours is a fishing town. Almost all of the families around Maliseet Lake make their living fishing for charr and receiving government subsidies for fishing. The rest earn a living working at establishments necessary to support the town: the bait shop, barber shop, grocery store, diner, boat repair, bank, etc. I teach at Maliseet High School. Forty-six students total.

"People are still going to send their kids to school," I say.

But I am wrong. At eight-fifteen, the doors are still locked. There is no note. The principal has assumed that word about the lake would spread. I turn around. The day is bright and lovely. It is warm for April in Maine. Trees are beginning to bud. I let my jacket fall open as I walk.

I go straight to the community center, which is already filling up at eight-thirty. Smith and Peter are sitting together near the front. I find an open seat in the next row.

"Hey," I say.

Smith says, "Nobody there, huh?"

I do not respond. "Has anything happened yet?"

"No," Smith says. He looks at his watch. "Not yet."

I listen to the people as they move around me, checking in. "Your boat?" They ask each other. Usually a nod or shaking of the head suffices as a response. Sometimes they elaborate. "Dented," I overhear, and "Fucked." These are not long-winded people.

Jackson calls the meeting to order at nine sharp. "Attention!" The roar fades to a whisper. "As I'm sure you all know, there has been a tragedy. Maliseet Lake is gone."

"We know!" the crowd exclaims. They peal off into shouts of "What happened?" and "What do we do?"

Jackson quiets them with a flash of his palms. He opens the floor for townspeople to come up one at a time and talk about their feelings and concerns.

About fourteen people speak—mostly fishers. They want to know what happened, how they will make their living now, and if the government is going to cut off their subsidies. For most, these subsidies come in the form of coupons for fuel, bait and other supplies. For some, it is monthly checks. This is to encourage our fishers to keep fishing even though the charr population of our lake is sadly depleted, more so every year. Jackson assures the fishers that, as city councilman, he has already contacted our state representative to ask about the subsidies.

Fred, who owns the bait shop, takes the floor to make a plea for his own livelihood. "Folks," he begins, "I know I usually see you for bait and line and such. But I hope you'll still come by the shop, even though there's no more fishing to be done. Until we get this whole thing straightened out at least."

People move in their seats. I hear an occasional cough, the crushing of a paper coffee cup.

Fred goes on, "Matty, two mornings ago you came in for line, but you also bought a mess of Powerbars and some shoe polish and a rawhide for Specks. Right? And George, you came in for lures and left with cigarettes, lighter fluid, and, um, something else. I won't say it. You know what I mean. So folks, all of you, I hope you'll remember that Davis' Bait isn't just bait. We got a load of other stuff you all need, too. Please don't stop coming to see me."

Juliette Mills steps up next with a plan to fill the lake back up. "If we all just bring in a couple of buckets from our bathtubs, we can fill it back in. There's three hundred some of us here, right? That's like, six hundred bucketfuls. That's a lot of water."

It is a sad day, so no one laughs. Juliette's heart is in the right place, even if her head isn't.

"Is that enough water?" she asks. "How much is enough?" After a long moment of silence, she sits back down next to Bill, and he puts his arm around her shoulders.

The floor stays empty for a minute or two and Jackson steps up to close out the meeting. "Okay then," he says. "Thank you to everyone who shared their feelings. I wrote down all of your concerns and I'll take them up with our state rep. Hopefully he'll get back to us quickly. Everyone just sit tight until then. I'll call another meeting just as soon as I have word."

People start to move towards the bathrooms, the exits, or a final cup of coffee when Annette from the barbershop stands to speak.

"This is a sign from God," she says. "I'm sure of it. Some of you haven't been doing what you should be doing and this is God punishing all of you. He took away our lake." She turns her attention to Father Clark near the coffee urns. "You know it's true, Father. This is His work."

Before Jackson can usher her off the floor, she ushers herself off. She walks down the center of the hall like a fashion model and through the big doors before anyone says another word.

····

Things stay quiet until the protestors arrive on Saturday. Among the madness, we'd forgotten to expect them. They've been coming off and on for over a year, Saturdays at seven a.m. They come to protest the fishing subsidies with big black and white signs that say things like: "Fishing Subsidies Destroy Our Lakes!," "Keep Maine Alive!," and "Fishing Subsidies Hurt Everyone!" Many of the signs have drawings of charismatic fish. Some of the fish wear bowties or top hats. When I look at the signs I wonder if any of these people have seen an actual fish. There are usually ten or twelve protestors, not always the same ten or twelve, and they have singled out our lake as an example of what they say fishing subsidies are doing to lakes all over Maine.

We watch them get off the bus, towing their big signs. One of them points at the crater and shouts and then like a ripple on water they all see it. Smith and I are outside having coffee. We leave our steaming mugs on the porch rail and approach the protestors.

"Why are you shits here?" Smith asks.

"When did this happen?" asks a man with a sign.

"Thursday," I say. "Or Wednesday night I guess." None of us are sure when the lake disappeared. A few of the townsfolk claim to have heard a rushing sound, like the flushing of a giant toilet, in the night. But even they admit it could have been a train passing through the hills.

"Where's your precious charr now?" Smith asks. "Gone or dead. And no one even got to eat 'em. No more fishing here. Happy?"

They are not happy. Some of them are even crying.

"You should tell people about this," the man says.

"Our councilman sent a letter to our state rep," I say.

"No, the news and stuff. You should get the news here."

"Do we get paid for being on the news?" Smith asks.

"No. But if people hear about this, they'll want to help you guys. Are you, like, fucked now or what?"

Smith spits in the dirt where the man has set his sign. He stomps toward Peter's house, three down from ours.

"I'm sorry," I say to the man. "We're all upset. Do you think you guys could go now? There's really nothing to protest anymore. Just go have breakfast or something?"

The group moves toward their cars and I run to Peter's. Inside, the men are talking about calling the local newspaper.

"Don't you get a reward for reporting the news?" Smith asks.

"I think that's only if they're looking for a bank robber," Peter says.

"I saw something on the news once," I say, "where this couple lost their house in a fire. And they had like five children. And a baby. And they put an address on the screen where people could send money to help them and I read later that they got like twenty-thousand dollars and put a down payment on a new house and bought their baby a new crib and everything."

Peter and Smith look at each other.

"If we don't call, those ratty protesters probably will. They've been trying to get the news here the whole time anyway," Peter says.

Smith picks up the phone.

••••

The first reporter comes that afternoon. He's from *The Sun Press* and carries a small spiral-top notebook. As soon as he sees the empty lake, he makes a phone call. Ten minutes later, three more reporters and a photographer are milling around the lake, knocking on doors, asking questions. At four, television crews appear. They talk to a bunch of us and ask a few if they'd like to be on camera. Fred from the bait shop says no until they tell him he can mention the name of his store, which he has changed from Davis' Bait to Davis' Market. He gives a short interview, along with a few others.

Annette from the barbershop stands silent in her doorway. These days she doesn't talk to anyone. She spends the mornings walking laps around the lake, worrying rosary beads, chanting softly to herself.

The reporters thank us and leave to prepare for the six o'clock news. A few of us gather at Peter's to watch it together. We clap loudly when Jackson appears, gesturing to the empty lake. The video shots are mostly close-ups of trash, the skeletons of dead fish picked clean by the birds, broken boats. It looks like a giant garbage dump in the center of our town. The group around me cheers, but I feel ashamed. We should have taken better care of the lake. And now, even though it's gone, we should have at least cleaned up the crater.

More news crews come back the next day. And so do the protestors. There are more of them than ever, and they all have signs.

"See what fishing subsidies do!" they yell.

"They destroy the environment!"

"Fishing subsidies ruin Maine's lakes!"

The townspeople yell from the other side of the lake. "We didn't do this!"

"This has nothing to do with our subsidies!"

"Go away!"

I keep a watchful eye out for Annette. I expect her to add her theory about God and His great punishment, the reverse flood, into the mix. But she does not appear.

••••

After a week, visitors to the lake no longer surprise us. In addition to the protestors and news crews, a swarm of scientists has come to investigate.

"No apparent fissures," they whisper into their tape recorders. "No new tributaries that might account for loss of water volume."

They cannot tell us what happened, but some fishers in a nearby river have reported catching charr where there was no charr before.

There are other visitors, too. People from all over Maine, all over the Northeast have come to look at the disappearing lake. We watch them from our porches, like circus people. They take photographs and lead their children around by their sticky hands. Fred starts stocking candy and small toys in the bait shop. He sells out of giant suckers.

The lake has taken on a life of its own. The bottom is covered in a thick carpet of grass. Some small plants have sprung up. Helen from the bank plants tomatoes where her husband used to tie his boat. "This is real fertile soil," she says. "We should fill the lake with tomatoes. Make our money back."

Smith responds with venom, "We can't get no tomato subsidies, Helen."

The only thing that hasn't changed is the level of fear in our town. Fred has to throw away four hundred dollars worth of live bait that has gone bad. The fishers have missed two Monday markets. They sit twiddling their thumbs from four to nine every morning. None of them can sleep in. The students in my English class write stories in which a monster from the woods drinks up all the lake water, burps out the trash, and disappears back into the forest. There is still no official word about our subsidies, but the checks have stopped coming.

This is the atmosphere when the first church group arrives at Maliseet Lake on a Sunday. There are four of them: three women and a man. The women are in long, earth-toned dresses. The man wears a priest's collar and holds a Bible. They pray quietly. Annette brings them lemonade and stands with them for a while. She speaks, gesturing wildly, and the priest listens, nods, and puts a hand on her elbow. Before they leave, he pulls something from the crater. It is the handle from someone's broken tackle box. He puts it his pocket and the four of them leave.

Smith, next to me on the porch, breaks into a wide smile. "Town meeting!" he yells. "We're having a town meeting! Everyone get to the Community Center! Ten minutes!"

"Smith," I ask, "what?"

"Ten minutes," he says. "Tell everyone."

••••

Only about a third of the town shows up to the meeting and there is no coffee. Smith takes the floor.

"Hi everyone," he says. "Good morning."

A voice emerges from the crowd, "What's going on, Smith?"

"I have an idea of how we can still make our living from the lake without our subsidies."

The chatter dies down.

Smith continues, "There's all these people here now. They're all walking around looking at the lake. And, yeah, sometimes they buy soda or whatever from Fred and get lunch at the diner and buy gas. But I think we could really make some money off of them. I saw that priest out there take a broken tackle box handle from the lake. Those religious people think the lake is blessed."

Jonah from the diner asks, "You want to charge them admission to see the lake?"

"No," Smith says. "Then they'd stop coming. I want to charge them for everything else. Souvenirs and stuff."

"Postcards?"

"T-shirts!"

"Coffee mugs!"

"Yeah, all that kind of stuff," says Smith. "But then expensive stuff, too. Like, that handle the priest took? That's trash. But now we can probably sell the lake trash for a lot of money."

"Who's going to want to buy garbage?"

"A lot of people. People think it's a miracle what happened here. I saw on the news that some guy sold a cheese sandwich on the internet for forty thousand dollars because it looked like it had Jesus on it. We got a whole supply of this stuff. Miracle stuff. And when we run out of junk, we can sell pieces of the lake. Like, little bottles of lake dirt."

I listen while Smith and a few others shout back and forth pricing soda cans and fishing lures and pieces of boats. It is a great idea, even if it seems a little like ripping people off. It never occurred to me that people would spend money to buy trash out of our lake. But that's the difference between Smith and me, he's always thinking about people that have more money than he does.

Smith and nine others form a committee to take charge of the new business. Jonah wants to call it "the miracle committee" but the group settles on "tourism." They decide the money should be split evenly among the fishers and anyone else who lost income from the lake. Everyone who plans to take a cut has to help: gathering "relics" from the crater, bottling dirt, sending out fliers to Maine churches, or manning the souvenir shop, which will replace the old fishing supplies part of Davis' Market.

• • • •

The people of Maliseet are industrious and within a month Davis' Souvenir Shop is up and running. The postcards are unpacked. They showcase photos by Layla Wilkins, a retired dance teacher in town. My favorite shows the sun setting over the Maliseet crater. The angle is low enough that if you look quickly, you might think the lake wasn't gone at all.

There are t-shirts, too. One says, "I swam in Maliseet Lake" and has a drawing of a frowning man standing in a dry lakebed.

My students at Maliseet High design tags to go on the relics. We attach them with loops of twine. "Maliseet Lake," they say. "The Disappearing Lake. Maine."

People who saw our lake on the news come to visit. They send postcards to five friends and their five friends come. Then they each send five postcards and twenty-five more people come. Plus their families. We are soon overrun with tourists. Jimmy and Julie who ran a boat repair shop turn their space into a makeshift bed and breakfast. Their four rooms are full every night. Others follow suit. The land around us is bought up quickly. Best Western puts in a bid on a tract of land two miles from the lake. McDonald's buys a plot. There are bulldozers and Coming Soon signs everywhere. But for now, it is just us and we are doing very well. We sell out of lake trash in one month. The last thing to go is a fiberglass boat, its smashed engine pieces included. It sells for two thousand dollars and the pee-wee football team gets new uniforms. Helen from the bank shows us how we can cut out pieces of land from the bottom of the lake in three-inch by three-inch squares. With the bright grass, they look nicer than the bottles of dirt and sell better, too, at five bucks a pop. Squares with flowers or the beginnings of trees sell for three times as much. We are pulling more money out of the lake now than we ever did fishing charr.

But not everyone is happy. Peter wakes up to a woman in a lime windbreaker taking pictures in his kitchen. Tourists trample Helen's tomatoes. The traffic in and out of town is brutal. And Annette, lonely Annette, stages her own small protest of the relic sale.

On Tuesday, I bring her coffee on my way to school. She stands on the church steps with her arm threaded through the handle of the collection basket. She hands out fliers to passing tourists. They say: "The church is God's house, not the lake. We are being punished for our sins by the disappearance of our lake. Everyone must pray! Please donate to our church."

When I stop to pick up my thermos on the way home, Annette is sitting with her head in her hands.

"Get any visitors today?" I ask.

She shakes her head. "They spend all their money on pieces of grass. I don't understand."

"You should help us," I say. "You could give your share to the church if you want."

"I will not. This is wrong what you are doing. God is trying to tell us something and you shouldn't be making money from it. This is serious."

"People are just trying to make back what they've lost." As I say it, I realize it is no longer true. The town is changing. Fred has a flat screen T.V. he didn't have before. Julie bought a new Land Rover. Many of my students have cell phones and jeans with designer labels. Smith and I have put our money away. We don't talk much about what we'll do with it, but we like knowing it is there. I put a dollar in the basket.

"You should think about it," I say. "Maybe it's not such a bad thing. Everyone is doing alright."

On the way home, I go by the lake. It is changing, too. The topography of its bottom has been re-carved in three-inch by three-inch sections. The grass begins to grow back in some places; others are still bare. In two weeks, school will be out and it will be swimming season. What will the children do, I wonder, to keep themselves out of trouble?

••••

By late August the number of tourists in our town is dizzying, but our steady stream of income has waned to a trickle and begun to dry up. The visitors can now stay at the Best Western outside of town. And they do. They eat at McDonald's and buy their souvenirs at the Shirt Shack on the highway. The Shirt Shack sells grass from the back of their parking lot in three-inch by three-inch squares. They call it "Maliseet grass" and no one knows the difference. Our postcards fade in their metal racks. Coffee mugs gather dust. Squares of grass whither and die on Fred's shelves. A family of moles has moved into the lake crater. Our people are running out of money.

And now that they aren't spending money here, the tourists are more than a nuisance. They are a plague. They leave trash everywhere, knock on our doors to use our bathrooms, disrupt our thoughts with their noisy cars and even noisier children. They want us to take their pictures, standing in the lake, holding their noses as if underwater. Some of us do. Some of us don't.

School is set to start in a week and no one has money for supplies. Fred has sold his flat screen T.V. for a third of what he paid. There is a growing consensus that we need to get these people out. Jackson Stoat calls a town meeting. Everyone comes, including seven or eight tourists who nearly have to be forcibly removed. When they are gone, Jackson opens the floor.

"Can't we make them leave?" someone asks.

"No," says Jackson. "We really can't. We can keep them off our lawns and personal property, but that's it. They're allowed to come to the lake."

"Is there anything we can do?"

"There is," Jackson says. "Given a proper majority, the town can move to make changes, big changes, to itself. Remember five years ago when we wanted to build that new dock on the South side of the lake? We voted on it and most of us agreed and we built it? We could do that again."

"Build a dock?"

Jackson replies, "Fill in the lake."

The crowd boils. "You want to fill in our lake? With dirt?"

"I think it's the best thing to do under the circumstances. We'll rent some equipment, level some hills and use the dirt to fill in the lake. No lake, no tourists. There's nothing to be done with it now. It's a giant hole in the ground."

"How will we make money?" asks Lee, a fisher's wife. She's sent her kids to live with their grandparents for a while. They have been thinking of selling their home.

"We should take it one step at a time," Jackson answers, "but I was thinking we might take advantage of the new space and, maybe, keep bees."

"Bees!" The noise from the crowd is a mix of laughter and anger. A handful of people walk out. Some listen in stunned silence as Jackson presents charts on the yearly profits of the bee-keeping industry.

"For a small investment," he concludes, "we could be back making more than we were fishing charr. We should put the space to good use. The lake isn't making anyone any money now. And nothing keeps away the tourists like bees!"

Annette stands, her head rising above the sea of seated faces like a ghost from a body. "What makes you think you can fill the lake in?"

No one responds. The room quiets as she walks to the front.

"The water didn't stay. What makes you think dirt will stay? God did this for a reason and you all want to bury it? So that others can make the same mistake? Let them come," she says. "Let them see. Maybe someone will learn a lesson and take it back to their town. God knows it's not happening here."

She pulls herself through the crowd on long legs and moves through the front door like a whisper. When the town's attention is focused on Jackson again, I slip out and follow her.

••••

"Annette!" I find her perched on her front porch swing. "What is it that you think we did?"

She doesn't say anything.

"You must think we did something really awful if God is punishing us this much. What is it? What did I do, Annette? What did you do?"

I can see that she is crying a little, and it makes me soften.

"I don't know," she says. "I've been trying to figure it out. When it first happened, I looked around and only saw goodness and good things. Our people work hard. They raise their kids. They do their best. But there must be a reason."

"How do you know?"

"Because there has to be! It's just too awful!" She puts her hands in her pockets. Perhaps fingering a rosary in one of them. "Maybe we were being tested, but we handled it all wrong. You guys were all taking money from those people who just wanted to come and see what we see every day. And then the companies came in and, serves you all right, took it away. I don't think it's going to work now, anymore, for this town. I think it's all over."

"So you're leaving?"

"No," she says. "I'm staying. God will have to send a tornado and blow me out."

••••

Instead of going home, where I know Smith will be waiting to talk about the meeting and the bees and tell me what we should do next, I go to the lake. I hope for a quiet moment to reflect, but the place is crawling with people in sun visors and khaki shorts. Some of the town is there, too. Jackson and three others, fishers turned relic-sellers, are already putting the bee plan into action, surveying what they can level. In a year this town will have lost one lake and one hill. The new landscape will be filled with bee boxes and For Sale signs.

Already, our people are suffering. There is the money,

yes, but not only the money. There is also Annette's despair, Fred's rotten bait, Helen's trampled tomatoes. Our men's hands twitch around imaginary fishing poles. At night we watch bobbers dip below the borders of our eyelids and wake up wet, in lakes of our own sweat. We crave the feeling of cool water on our dry skin.

I want to take something to remember Maliseet Lake by. We have stopped being able to sell pieces of the lake, so the bottom is covered with unruly grass and weeds: sharp edged green things, dandelion puffs, skinny white mushrooms in shady spots. I cut myself a square, three-inches by three-inches, of dirt and grass. It is not the lake, I know, but it is all I have left.

Cheater
• • • • • • • • •

Alex's apartment looks like a hotel room after the guests have gone to checkout. There are towels on the floor and dirty wine glasses around. The bedspread came with the sheets, came with the curtains, came with the throw pillows on the couch. A complete set. The fireplace is fake. There is only generic art on the walls. No photographs. No real trace of a permanent personality. Maybe Alex is a different man with every girl he brings home. Or maybe there is no real Alex. Or maybe he just doesn't care to decorate. I tend to think people have more depth than they really do.

When I wake up the first time, the sun is nowhere in sight. So I think it'll be okay if I go back to sleep for a little while. But when I wake up again the sun has pounded its way through the shades, dropped to the floor, crawled across the carpet, over my clothes, up onto the bed and into my hair.

I am already in a terrible mood when I gather my clothes. Luckily, it is a Saturday, so I'm not late for work. Alex is still asleep as I start to get dressed. After too many mornings spent searching in vain for my stockings, I stopped wearing them to pick up guys. So now it's my wedding ring I'm looking for when I realize that I've forgotten to take it off again.

I wake Alex up to tell him I'm leaving. He says okay and doesn't even roll over before he goes back to sleep. He stopped offering me cabs a long time ago.

April in Pittsburgh is schizophrenic. Sometimes it feels like December. Today, it feels like August. I try to read the Post-Gazette on the bus back to Squirrel Hill, but my head is brimming over with stories about last night and no one to tell them to. I'd never done it in a bar before. But when I replay the scene under my eyelids all I can see is that little band of gold on my fourth finger. My clothes feel heavy and out of place, like they've soaked up a little of Alex's apartment. Maybe I have, too; I feel a little generic.

By the time I get off the bus, I have taken my mind off of the bar and focused it on how badly I need a shower. I spot Evan across the street. I don't know his real name, but he looks like an Evan. I can walk for blocks on autopilot without ever taking in the scenery, but I never miss Evan, even in a crowd. He's on his way to work and I curse myself for going back to sleep at Alex's. He has a folded copy of the paper in one hand and with the other he is idly twisting the little gold band mine is designed to match. I wonder if he notices me. For a second I almost feel a connection. I imagine that the rest of his paper's sitting on the kitchen table next to my clean coffee mug. I ignore that fact that I wake up at my own place so seldom that I don't even get a paper delivered there anymore.

When I get to my apartment, I notice that my clothes are

starting to smell like me again, but my bag still reeks like stale cigar smoke and the Irish shower I took at Alex's. Figures. It's the only piece of my outfit I can't wash. I bet a real designer bag would blend seamlessly from life to life. The second I came back it would smell like vanilla-scented candles and carpet that's been vacuumed too often. Instead, it reminds me of the Squirrel Cage and how I had to try and clean up the mess between my thighs with cocktail napkins. They were the brown, recycled kind with the name of the bar screened onto them. The ink left little black streaks on my legs. Plus, I was sore and they were scratchy, but Alex was hissing at me to hurry up because the bartender was giving us looks. We got out of there and I tried to lighten things up a little by saying "thanks" and flashing him a secret smile. He ignored me until we got into his car and he asked if I was on the pill.

After my shower and a shot of Febreeze to my bag, I try to meet Evan for lunch, but he doesn't show up at the Murray Avenue Grill at the usual time. Instead, he ambles in just as I am leaving. I open my lips to say something, but he walks past.

It is moments like these that ruin my fun, when Evan refuses to play along. I know he isn't really my husband. He's just someone I noticed on the street once and followed to work. And then home. Then to where he eats. And shops. I bought a ring that looked like his and inserted him into my fantasy. Because I don't have anyone to cheat on. And I love the rush. It makes me feel dangerous and exciting, and I am neither of those things without it. So I tell myself that it is worth the work I have to do in these moments. I reinvent the exchange. In my mind: I opened my lips to try and explain, but he mistook it for a smile and walked away.

••••

I wake up on Kevin's couch at six a.m. He isn't next to me; I didn't expect him to be. I look for him in the bedroom, but

122

he isn't there either. Even though the sun is still low enough to cling to the ceiling and not the floor, both sides of the bed are cold. I try the kitchen and the shower before I accept that he's gone and start to get myself together. My wedding ring is in my empty champagne glass and most of my clothes are still on from the night before.

We'd met at Fanattics, a sports' bar, where I'd pretended to cheer for his hometown basketball team and he took me home with him. He led me away from the bedroom, saying his girlfriend would smell me on the sheets. We did it on the couch, which is plastic, treated to look like leather. I had to spread my jacket down under my bare legs and constantly rearrange myself to keep from sticking to it. It was less than comfortable, but the champagne we spilled and anything that leaked out of the condom were easy to wipe up afterwards. I only felt a little unsanitary when I woke up with my mouth pressed against the pleather. The sex was good. I was drunk enough to be loud and he was drunk enough not to notice that I was leaving the "K" off of his name.

I walk around his apartment once, slowly. I tell myself I'm making sure I haven't left anything; but when I start to look around rooms I was never in, I realize I'm looking for some kind of goodbye. Or some sort of affirmation that I was close to someone the night before, even for a little while. I don't find anything.

I was drunk when we left the bar, so I have no idea which bus to take home from Kevin's building. Luckily, he bought the drinks and I have just enough money to cab home on.

The cab ride is my first chance to think about how I feel. I have come down completely from the night before, and I start to think about grade school when they taught us about drugs. My hair is crunchy from dried champagne that the couch didn't soak up and my legs feel sunburned from peeling them off the plastic. I can still taste Kevin's hair gel under my fingernails when I bite them. My bag smells like champagne

123

and pine tree air freshener. I am glad I cannot smell my heart. Seven a.m. is not a good time for me. Maybe I am going through some kind of withdrawal.

I try to focus on the positive. The cool thing about sleeping with different people is the constant string of surprises. Kevin, for instance, started reciting the Our Father about twenty minutes in and didn't stop until he came. There will probably be a time when I find that creepy, but for now I am fascinated.

By the time I get to my apartment it's too late to catch Evan on his way to work. After an hour or so of doing nothing I start to feel transparent, like I'm bleeding into the wallpaper. So I shower and get the hell out of there. I don't realize where I'm going until I hit Shady Avenue. Then, I instinctively walk toward Evan's office building. Maybe it's because I feel guilty. Examining my motivations doesn't seem important.

Evan is outside on a cigarette break, a stubby Parliament looks ready to drop from his fingers. He looks right through me and I think, "wallpaper."

"Hey."

"Hello," he says.

I can't find any emotion in his voice at all.

"I'll make this fast, I know you've got work to do. I was thinking maybe we could have dinner later in the week."

He looks confused and glances over his right shoulder.

"I think I'm busy," he says, and gestures to his wedding band.

My hand instinctively goes to mine. I can't find anything between us at all. His eyes look dead and I take a second to wonder if I've killed this. I try as hard as I can to think of the perfect thing to say, but I've got the Our Father stuck in my head and I can't think of anything at all.

I walk back to the bus stop slowly and start to worry about my fantasy fading. I have a pretty safe cure for times like these.

I buy things for Evan. Then I look at them and I can feel him in my apartment again. I stop into CVS and buy him a green toothbrush. I stop into Little's Shoes and buy him an expensive pair of boots. I stop into Orr's and buy him a new watch. By the time I stop home to drop his things off, I feel much better. I can't wait to go to the Squirrel Cage later. I imagine telling Evan I am heading to a meeting and I'll be there late.

••••

When I wake up, Mark is making breakfast. I quickly tie my hair back and throw on some lip gloss before I walk into the kitchen. I can hear the bacon frying before I can smell it.

"Smells good," I say.

"I'm sorry," he says, "I didn't make enough. I figured you'd be leaving."

"Oh," I say. "I am."

My stomach starts to hurt as I drag it away from the bacon smell. I think it's mad at me for filling it with so much alcohol. Fucking tequila sunrises; they're so pretty.

My clothes are thrown over a chair in the bedroom. There's nothing to look around for and no reason I can think of to prolong my visit. Not that I really want to, I just hate that surreal feeling I get on the way home: "Did that really happen?" My imagination's so good these days. Sometimes it's hard to tell. Luckily Mark's apartment smells like kitty litter and my skirt probably does, too.

Mark's house is small, but charming. The border on the wallpaper is matched up perfectly which makes me think he has a girlfriend, even though he swore he doesn't. The furniture looks like college leftovers. There are desk chairs where there should be recliners, futons where there should be couches, beer cans where there should be vases. He called it his "bachelor pad" but it doesn't have Foosball, so I don't think it counts.

The sex was unremarkable. Even when I thought he was making me breakfast, it didn't seem that great. Every time I got close he would pull back and prompt me to beg for it. I did a half-assed job just to get things going, but I wasn't into it. I also thought he got too sweaty. I was tempted get up half way through and switch on the ceiling fan, but I figured that would make it last longer, and at that point I just wanted to get to sleep.

By the time we finished, I was sober again and getting restless. He passed out right away and I stayed up for a little while. I wanted to know something about him. I didn't need his life story, or even his telephone number. Just something to make him feel like a real person. I walked around searching for the Foosball table. Nothing. I checked his fridge to see if maybe he was a vegetarian. Nope. I looked through his wallet for photos, but I didn't find any. I learned his eye color from his driver's license and went back to bed.

On the way home I slip into withdrawal again. I feel sweaty and laced with doubt. I smell my skirt for evidence of last night. Kitty litter. I stop thinking about how delusional I might be and puzzle over why I never saw a cat.

The tequila makes my stomach feel like it's closing in on itself. I look through the cupboards to find something to prop it up with, but the only thing I have a taste for is bacon. I head to Pamela's, best breakfast in the 'burgh.

Evan is there with some woman I don't recognize. I watch them flirt back and forth for a little while, but I don't worry until he leans over to kiss her. Then I walk past, letting my heels click loudly, which I never do.

He doesn't look over. Neither of them follows me with their eyes. Their right hands are clasped across the table and the fingers on their left hands are looped through the handles on their coffee mugs. I can see their matching wedding bands. Hers looks more expensive than mine and she wears it under a diamond solitaire. They look right together. I don't notice I've stopped to stare until Evan, or whatever his name is, looks over. I fake a yawn to hide the tears in my eyes, but he doesn't notice them anyway.

I storm out of the diner thinking some combination of "maybe I'll buy him that expensive bathrobe" and "now I've gone too far." I hover over a sewer grate outside the restaurant and pull my ring from my finger. The skin is a little lighter underneath it and the feel of skin brushing skin there is foreign and unpleasant. I know Evan and I are over. I can't fix that. I struggle to tell myself: he didn't treat me right. I'm filing for divorce. But I know I won't feel like my dangerous, exciting self again until I'm remarried, for better or for worse, for real or…not. I palm my wedding ring, and carefully tuck it into my purse on the ride home.

••••

The next weekend I need an adventure, so I go to Silky's. It's mostly Pitt students watching the Penguins game, so wouldn't usually be my pick, but it's ladies' night and my drinks are free. On the way in I get a plastic cup and a black stamp on the back of each hand. I say a silent prayer that they'll fade by Monday. I take a look at my options. Too young, too short, too skinny, not in a million years, out of my league, maybe if I was drunk enough, and then I see him: Perfect. He's too old to be here, at least forty, and when I glance over, a sorority girl is giving him a dirty look and storming off. I know he's not having any luck and think that maybe he's as desperate as I am to get laid. I make eye contact from across the bar and sit down next to him, our legs touching. He offers me a drink and I display my ladies' night stamps. He smiles.

He asks if I'm married.

I tell him, "We're working on a divorce."

Pittsburgh scores on the television over his right shoulder.

He is drinking Guinness, so I am too, but I have a hard time getting it down. I look around at the few college girls with their pastel drinks in plastic cups.

He tells me he was married once.

"Didn't like it?"

He shakes his head.

The Guinness starting to settle in my stomach and flutter to my brain.

He tells me his name is Rick.

"Pleasure to meet you," I say, drawing out the L so he'll think about my tongue.

The music from the jukebox is so loud I can't feel my heartbeat over the bass line.

He tells me I have beautiful eyes.

"Rick," I ask, leaning in a little, "are you hitting on me?"

The barstools are too high and my feet are dangling a couple of inches above the floor. It makes me feel silly and I'm anxious to get out of here, but he orders us another round.

He asks what we should drink to.

I raise my plastic cup, "Marriage."

And we drink.

Two hours, three pints of Guinness, sixteen jam band songs, a short uphill walk and two flights of stairs later, he's fumbling with the keys to his place and I'm squeezing his ass through his work pants. I hear the lock click and help him turn the doorknob. As soon as we get inside, he backs me up against the wall and slips his hand between my legs. The faded blue color of the room reminds me of the backgrounds on Saturday morning cartoon shows. In my head, the Looney Tunes theme song is the soundtrack to the rest of the evening.

When I wake up, Rick is walking out the door. I dress quickly and follow him from a safe distance. I don't know where we're walking to, but on the way there I slip on my ring and start to think about our wedding. At first I can't decide where we had it, or how many bridesmaids there were.

But the more I think about it, the clearer it becomes in my mind: Rick's spontaneous wide-eyed proposal, our rehearsal dinner on Mount Washington, how mad I was when he dropped his wedding ring in the drain and lost it, how he'd never suspect any infidelity on my part, how we're so in love.

This is my second husband, Rick. The green toothbrush in my bathroom is Rick's. I like the sound of it already. Rick steps into a Dry Cleaner's on Forbes. When thirty minutes go by and he still hasn't emerged with a couple of shrink-wrapped shirts or an off-season jacket, I copy the address into my date book labeling it, "Rick's job." I walk down the street quickly. I have work to do. I have a whole life to create and only twelve hours to do it in. I have to hurry if I'm going to be at the bar by nine.

Why We Never Talk About Sugar

●●●●●●●●●●●●●●●●●●●●●●●●●●●●●●●●●●●●●

The first stories came out of France. Paris, actually—the city of love. There were three of them in rapid succession. A bloated brunette appeared in the paper under the headline: *French Woman Pregnant With Diamond Watch.* I read them with my sister, whose own empty uterus weighed her down, kept her balled up on the sofa. A few days later we read another headline: *Second French Women Pregnant With Object.* This article was accompanied by a grainy ultrasound. The object inside her was small, rectangular, and solid. Six months later, the headline read: *French Woman Gives Birth to Four Squares of Dark Chocolate.* By then, the strange pregnancies were everywhere.

While the details remained mysterious, scientists and poets agreed that reproduction had become divorced from sex, and now required only love. And since DNA was out of the equation, women were at risk of conceiving anything they loved. In the best of cases, the things were small: a handful of fabric covered buttons, a miniature ceramic panda, a pair of jade earrings. Morning sickness aside, these pregnancies didn't cause much discomfort. The weight gain was minimal, the births were easy.

But sometimes there was danger. A woman in California was ripped in half when her greedy husband finally convinced her of the lovable qualities of the Bentley GTC. A zookeeper in Montreal nearly died giving birth to a pair of Bengal tiger cubs.

"Aren't they beautiful?" my sister said, watching the zookeeper nuzzle her twins on the evening news.

"I don't know," I said. "We have to be careful now."

She continued to stare at the tigers as I averted my eyes, focusing instead on a brass floor lamp I had never liked. We were all learning to be careful. New courses on "Safe Love" were added to the high school curriculum when a rash of teen pregnancies swelled little girls up with bean bag toys, pop CDs, silky ballet slippers. "Not looking for love?" advertisers asked. "Buy this fair-to-middling book." "Try our nutritious, but bland line of ready-to-eat meals." "Listen to our special mix of mediocre music."

And we did, most of us. We kept our heads down. We learned to quiet our feelings. We pulled back our wandering hands, put down forks, never looked too long at art, or listened too closely to beautiful music.

Except my sister. One morning I walked in on her staring at a picture of her ex-husband, Alex, whispering, "I love you. I love you."

"Stop!" I yelled. "What are you doing?"

"I want a baby," she said.

"Like this?"

"Didn't I love Alex as much as those women loved shampoo samples and touch-screen cell phones?" She gestured to the paper, open to the week's birth announcements.

I left her alone with her photograph. I wanted to help, but it was too risky to talk about love.

Doctors stopped looking for a solution, instead women had to watch out for themselves. We learned not to love. Our flat bellies became a sign of our self-control. There were abortions, lots of them. At first, they were mostly for big things, dangerous things: palm trees, piles of fresh laundry, cherry wood rocking chairs. But more and more women decided that enduring the discomfort of pregnancy wasn't worth a piece of fried chicken or even the best-fitting bra. There were still girls with strange shapes in their bellies, but they walked slowly with shame on their faces. They knew it was their fault, what happened; they loved too easily.

Finally, after five years, the number of object births dwindled almost to nothing.

My sister was one of the last. After years of teaching herself to love in a world that was becoming increasingly loveless, she became pregnant with a set of antique sugar spoons, just like the ones our grandmother had when we were young. They jangled inside of her, poking her when she moved. Only when she lay on her right side with her knees up did they nest inside one another.

I waited in the hospital as she gave birth. They were small spoons; there wasn't much pain. She showed them to me after the doctor rinsed them off—eight in all. Their scalloped edges gleamed in the flat hospital light.

Now she keeps them in a box in the attic. I polish them once a year so she doesn't have to.

ACKNOWLEDGEMENTS

I will start by thanking my family, whose support and understanding makes it possible for me to write what is in my heart. And my husband, Devan, my best editor, who always sees great possibilities for my work and who isn't afraid to dream big.

Thanks also to Jeff Condran and Robert Peluso. Their keen editorial eyes have improved the manuscript considerably and their enthusiasm has made this process a joyful one.

I have been blessed with many fantastic writing teachers who lent me their expertise long after I left their classrooms. Their brilliance, generosity and dedication to their craft inspire me still. Chuck Kinder, Cathy Day and Kathleen George had important roles in making me the writer I am. Special thanks are due to Steven Hayward, who gave me the best writing advice I have ever received: You just have to write it.

Thanks to the editors who originally published these stories and, in some cases, improved them—especially to Roxane Gay, who has been a great supporter of my work and who is a terrific role model for any aspiring writer. And to Matt Bell for his generous endorsement of the book.

I am also supported in my endeavors by a broad community of fellow writers. Their bottomless talent and excitement for what we do push me to do my own best work.

Finally, I owe debts of gratitude to the University of Pittsburgh and the Colorado College for their material support, without which this book would not have been possible.